HIDDEN

USA Today Bestselling Author
Carmen Fox

The Silverton Chronicles

*(based on the novella of the same name, published in the 2017 Sigils
and Spells boxed set)*

SMART HEART
PUBLISHING

To Nana

WYWH

PROLOGUE

The moment when light fades into darkness is like an elixir for the soul. At night, the expectations of who we should be fall away. And what do I do with this precious freedom? I cower from it. I hide in financial records and the intricacies of tax legislation so my alpha can keep order without undue worry. It's who I am. Who I was. Until…

CHAPTER ONE

The stench of death batted me on the nose the second my foot struck the bottom stair. Darkness shrouded the entrance hall of our building, save for a sliver of moonlight from one of the windows, but I saw well enough to evade the bag Rollo had left standing by the door.

Someone, or something, shuffled outside.

I yanked open the door.

A blond white guy crouched over the body of a woman lying in the fetal position. The air above her was heavy with the smell of vinegar and mold, and a hint of impending rain.

A body.

On our doorstep.

The picture in front of me made no sense.

The guy snapped up his head and snarled, two canines protruding from his mouth.

"What the hell are you doing?" I pressed through gritted teeth.

Eli's eyes were the color of coal. Not a good sign.

I slammed the door shut. A vampire in the middle of a blood frenzy was one boot size too large, even for me.

A scratch on the door.

"Hey, dude." Eli whispered, then louder, "Ali. Where are you going?"

Fang boy spoke in coherent sentences? Now, that was odd. Once the frenzy took hold, their brain functions usually focused on food rather than on conversation.

I held my ear to the door. "What do you want?"

"Not sure if you noticed," Eli said, "but there's a dead chick outside your door."

"Do you have your blood frenzy under control?"

"What? Oh. No, there's no blood to trigger it. Besides, I haven't had one of those in weeks."

I slid open the door. "That's comforting."

"I've been doing spiritual yoga, and it's really helped."

A suave smile had replaced Eli's fangs. Our past interactions had rarely gone beyond a nod or a stiff 'all right,' so I had no reason to trust his charm offensive, but his brother, Florian Dupree, was a close friend. I simply couldn't believe Eli had killed the girl and placed her on our doorstep.

"You look confused." Eli's voice all but accused me of being slow on the uptake.

Maybe he was right.

The rest of my pack had retired to their rooms by eleven, and the last TV had fallen silent an hour ago. The same routine as most nights. This situation right here—body, vampire, small talk—this was not something I could have foreseen.

"Who is she?" I pointed my chin at the body. "And why is she outside my house?"

Long purple hair covered her face. Best I could tell, she was white. Her leather jacket was ripped, although it was impossible to say if by design or from an altercation.

"No idea." Eli rolled the woman onto her back. "I thought she was one of your wolves."

"Oh God." I gripped my thighs to keep from swaying.

For a few seconds, I stared, and in that time, emptiness filled my heart. My legs buckled. I stayed upright through sheer doggedness. The vampire, this stranger, would not see me weak over a trick of the mind. My vision tunneled to her face. This wasn't right. Heidi was too young, too alive, to have been claimed by death. No, she was upstairs in her room, asleep like the others. She *had* to be.

If it weren't for the beauty spot on her cheek…

I blinked through the threatening blindness to clear my vision and brain.

"That's Heidi. How…" I took a hitched breath. "I don't understand. How?"

Eli bent over and checked her eyes and neck before straightening again. "No wounds, no petechiae, or strangulation marks. Best guess, poison."

"What?" I jerked my gaze back to the door. Any minute now, the noise would wake Heidi, and she'd come padding down the stairs to complain. "What kind of poison? Who would poison her?"

"All good questions."

"Shit." I struck the doorframe with my palm, then went to check her pulse myself.

Her skin was purplish-gray and cold to the touch.

Eli was right. She was gone.

Numbness pounded my brain, forming an icy desert from which thoughts merely slipped into the abyss. When had she dyed her hair again? Had I neglected my duties? The sound of the door as Heidi was leaving should have alerted me. I just never thought she'd sneak out.

Except, there was precedence.

Two months ago, I'd caught her by the back door. She'd denied being up to anything, but of course I smelled the lies. Then she smiled and hugged me, and all of a sudden, telling my alpha about her transgression no longer seemed necessary.

"I need to get Parker." I pressed the heel of my hand into my right eye. "Damn."

Parker would know what to say. How to make things better. I was only the pack's second in command, in charge of accounts and enforcing the rules. Parker, by contrast, had this magical alpha calm about him that would help me focus.

"Don't tell him." Eli grabbed my shirtsleeve. "Please."

"What?" I stared. "Why?"

"Your dead werewolf is our business now."

"Are you crazy?" I yanked free from his grip.

Heidi's dead eyes glared up at me. Would her life have flashed by before her in those last seconds? What about the promise we'd made to keep her safe? The promise *I'd* made? Would she have remembered it in the end?

Eli retrieved a badge from his jacket pocket and flipped it open. "Eli Dupree. Assistant Director of the Interracial Enforcement Agency."

Hadn't he known my name just a minute ago? "I know. We've met. Like, six or seven times. I was at your brother's bonding ceremony. I had longer hair then?"

"Ah, yes." He gave a somber nod. "A very moving occasion."

Even at this hour of the night, a few birds made their presence heard. Their cuckooing held a mournful tone that struck straight at my heart.

"This is werewolf business." I massaged the pressure point on my right temple. "Parker will know what to do."

"I'm not kidding around, Ali. Your pack must stay out of this."

"Your agency has no authority over us."

"No, but unless you give me your word you won't involve Parker, I'm not going to tell you what I know about her death."

I rolled a fist but punched neither the wall nor him. "Who was it? Who killed her?"

"I see we're having communication problems." His smile twisted into a firm expression. "Let's keep her death between us for now, and I'll share my information with you. We'll pick up the killer together. You and I."

I was in no mood to play games over Heidi's death. The pack had a right to know. They might not have shared our bond, but she'd been precious to everyone.

"I can't do that." I backed away. "She isn't an interracial pawn you can use for whatever your agency has in mind. She's special. She *was* special, I mean."

A rock had formed in my lungs. It rolled left, shifted right, nudging me ever more out of my equilibrium. Why had this happened to Heidi when the world was full of bastards that deserved a one-way ticket to hell?

"I never met her." Eli's tone softened. "How old was she?"

"Barely nineteen."

"Tell me about her."

How could I cram her personality into words? My emotions were a jumble right now, whizzing through my guts, punching and jabbing. But once he knew who Heidi was, who she'd been, he might go away and leave us to our grief.

"There was that one day. Jim, our pack's fixer, got drunk and rowdy, so I asked him to leave." I shook my head, reliving the moment. "The dude built himself up in front of me and said, 'Make me.' Heidi, all eight years of her, blond hair in pigtails and chocolate clinging to her mouth, pushed her hands against her hips and called him a *meanie*. Then she declared me her brother, and that I was under *her* protection."

"She sounds fierce." Eli's gaze was focused.

"She was." I pressed my hand against my stomach, where waves of wretchedness poured into the hollow inside. "Many of us feel the need to protect our women because there are so few of them compared to males. But Heidi? She would have given the rest of the pack a run for our money, I can tell you that."

At last, my voice broke, forcing my mouth shut. Loss was a part of life. I understood that on an objective, cerebral level, but Heidi's absence was visceral. Palpable. Not least because she'd never get the chance to prove my prediction right.

If I'd been stricter with her, maybe she wouldn't have snuck out without telling us. Dammit, that's why we had rules and curfews. No unauthorized absences. Period.

Eli stood next to her crumpled shape, watching. Waiting.

"I can't let her death be covered by silence." I set my jaw tight and locked my back straight. "She deserves more."

"She deserves to be alive." Eli stepped around her body to block my view. "I can't change that. All I can do is deliver her killer. But I need the resources of my agency for that, and once you tell Parker, he'll want to take over."

Unlike his brother, Eli knew nothing of fashion. His jeans were straight from the eighties, and his brown leather jacket had seen better days. None of that mattered because his eyes drew my focus more than his clothes. Not for their light blue, but for their almond shape and their intensity. In his non-vamped-out state, they drilled into me with an impossible directness. Almost like a command to obey. In many ways, his choice of profession suited him. I'd spill my secrets like milk if he turned the screws on me.

"You realize you haven't spoken out loud in a while, right?" Eli winked—or maybe the low light had only made it seem that way. "Although I can see your brain's working overtime."

"Parker wouldn't approve. Hell, he'll demote me for even considering working with you and your agency."

"What if, when he wakes up in the morning, you break the news to him that you've already dealt with the killer? You'd be a hero. Not to mention how a quick resolution of this case might ease your pack's grief."

My life was neat and ordered. This situation was anything but. Maybe it wasn't me who was supposed to find them outside my house. This whole setup had to be a gigantic cosmic mistake.

"Maybe we should call your brother." I checked Eli's reaction, which barely registered. "He's the investigator. I'm not going to be any use to you."

"You'll do fine."

Curiously, his words didn't trigger my second nose, the sense that permitted me to smell lies.

The others would roll their eyes, of course. The idea of me breaking the rules was ludicrous. Besides, if I weren't around, who'd organize the Mourning? Still, Eli projected a certain amount of competence, and the unveiling of the killer could blast away this wretched confusion. If I could find meaning in Heidi's death, maybe everything would fall into its place.

Shit. He was one hell of a persuasive guy.

"Say I'm on board." I squinted. "What kind of help do you need?"

"First, we should remove your friend from your doorstep. Do you have a car?"

"Are you crazy?" My pitch went up, and I had to measure my breaths to calm down. "I'm not squashing Heidi into my trunk like last week's shopping. Forget it."

"I'm not going to *carry* her to our morgue." Eli pointed vaguely toward the road. "It's your car or a cab. Your choice, dude."

I pushed past Eli and crouched to stroke the hair away from her face. Her death had come too soon. I never got to tell her how important she was to me one last time. I didn't get to hold her close before she was torn from my life. Her eyes would never look at me again with love, only with empty resentment and blame.

What horrible deed could my girl have possibly committed that someone would do this?

I turned my head to the side to escape her reproach and his curiosity. "Why does she need to go to your facility at all?"

"Don't you want to know how she died?" Eli shifted his stance.

I peered up his length and then locked onto his gaze. Yes, I did. I wanted to know how she died very much. And then I wanted to dissect her killer and feed him his body parts until he choked. Or she. Could a woman be capable of such a crime?

"I have two conditions." I pushed myself up to standing. "No autopsy."

"That's doable. If this was poison, as I suspect, we'll only need to check her blood anyway. Magic will take care of the rest. What else?"

"How long do you think this will take? Parker gets up at seven."

"That gives us plenty of time to catch the killer."

I checked my pocket for my keys, then halted. "But you know who it was?"

"To be honest, I still need to cross the t's and dot the i's."

Could the pack find the murderer without Eli's help? Possibly, given enough time. But Eli had a head start. On any normal day, I'd say Rollo, our enforcer, would make a better hero in this situation. His practiced interrogations would go a long way in shaking loose leads. But what if, just this once, I tackled this situation on my own, rather than run to Parker? Heidi deserved at least that much from me. She'd been my family—maybe not by blood, but in every other way.

"Okay." I took a deep breath. "I'll work with you."

"Great. But just so you know, this is *my* show. Understood? I'm the one with the badge." He flipped it out again.

"I'm the one with the car." I dangled my fob from my fingers. "Shut up or call a cab. Your choice, *dude*."

Eli crossed his arms. "Think you're funny?"

I raised my eyebrows and cocked my head.

"Fine. I can be a team player." He slid his hands into the back pockets of his jeans. "Which car's yours?"

"Wait here." I slipped back inside the house and changed from my spotless loafers into walking boots that promised to be watertight, although I'd yet to test that theory. If the weather forecast was correct, I'd get a chance to find out tonight.

Heidi was dead. Three words that, on paper, carried almost no meaning, but inside me had opened a rift. Her off-color skin, the eyes that followed me around... I would find her killer, and I would make him pay.

"Come on. I don't have all night," Eli whisper-shouted.

I snatched my raincoat off the hook, closed the door behind me, and hurried after him. Eli had slung Heidi over his shoulder, her purple hair dangling down to his ass.

A gust of wind blew through the trees. Except for us, no one had ventured out tonight.

Our house was located in Custer Fields on the outskirts of Silverton—only two minutes away from Eli's home, which stood on the other side of the road. The glaring lights of downtown didn't reach this far out. Neither did its noise and bustle.

Eli glided silently through the blackness. Vampires had exceptional eyesight, while I had to rely on memory to find the way to the car without tripping over the steps or the grass strips that bordered our driveway.

Once upon a time, Eli and I would have been on opposite sides of a war, or even of a slice of toast—anything that could cause our two races to disagree. The modern world had civilized us, and most kin aspired to exist in harmony. His brother had settled successfully into our pack, even become a valuable part of the team.

Not all kin were as easy-going as Florian, of course, and those who didn't toe the line were dealt with by the Interracial Enforcement Agency. Except for us wolf packs, who lived outside the IEA's purview. We followed only our laws.

"Can you unlock your car?" Despite Eli's slim frame and the extra weight he carried on his shoulder, he hadn't lost any of the unmatched grace that his kind was known for.

When the Big Croupier in the Sky made the vampires and the werewolves, he dealt all the advantages to the fang brigade and hit us with the low cards. Not that I'd swap with Eli for anything. Vampires had their own shit to deal with.

When I pressed the unlock button, the lights of my Volvo

flashed. Eli had the trunk open and shut, with Heidi inside, before I'd even reached the car.

We climbed in, and I lifted my nose to catch the refreshing fragrance spreading inside. Eli's scent was reminiscent of ocean breeze and mint, with a touch of iron. Even my inner wolf approved of it, although I would have appreciated anything to drown out Heidi's death smell.

I had never gone against Parker's wishes, and while he'd never specified what I was to do in a situation such as this, stealing the body away in the middle of the night was one of those implied no-nos.

"Why aren't we taking your car?" I started the ignition and reversed out of my space. "You have one, don't you?"

"A Bugatti Veyron."

"Damn. That's a nice car."

"But not much room for a body. Besides, do you know how difficult it is to get the stink out of the carpet?"

"Can we please...?" I tightened my fists around the steering wheel. "Heidi is dead, man. She was a kid. Could you just...?"

"Not be an ass and show compassion?" Eli turned his head to the passenger window. "Sorry. Gallows humor. I see so much death in my job, you'd think I'd be used to it. Hell, I once produced my own share of corpses back in the day."

"Florian told me about your sire. Sorry he's dead."

"I don't wallow. I just meant I'm no longer that person. I finally appreciate and value the life of others."

How different we were. He was a blond, pale vamp with the lean grace of a cat, and I, a dark werewolf, built like a truck. I had never been able to simply shrug things off. More likely, they'd fester and eat at me until the next catastrophe came along.

"That's good to hear." I regarded Eli from the corner of my eyes. "Florian took your sire's death pretty hard."

He jerked his head around and bared his teeth. "I'm not my brother."

"Whoa." I raised an appeasing hand. "I didn't mean to say you were."

Due to circumstances beyond my control, a werewolf ritual had once linked my mind to Florian's. During that time, I got to know him better than I knew myself. That magical connection and that closeness were gone now, but getting rid of the memories proved much harder.

"Course not." Eli let his expression go blank, a blunt contrast to his tone, which was a brew of sarcasm and hurt. "I don't have Florian's charm, and *my* friend doesn't have superpowers. Fuck, I don't even have a friend. But I have a job to do, so let me concentrate on doing it. 'Kay?"

He crossed his arms, bumping his elbow against the door, and didn't even wince.

"'Kay." I overtook a hatchback that was hogging the center lane despite being the only other car around. "What part of your job are you concentrating on now?"

"The part that will tell me who killed your girl." He kept his gaze on the road.

I pushed the indicator down with more force than necessary. "I was under the impression you at least had an inkling of who that might be."

"I think I do."

"Care to enlighten me?"

"I think, and by this I mean I'm pretty sure, that Heidi may have been killed by a serial killer."

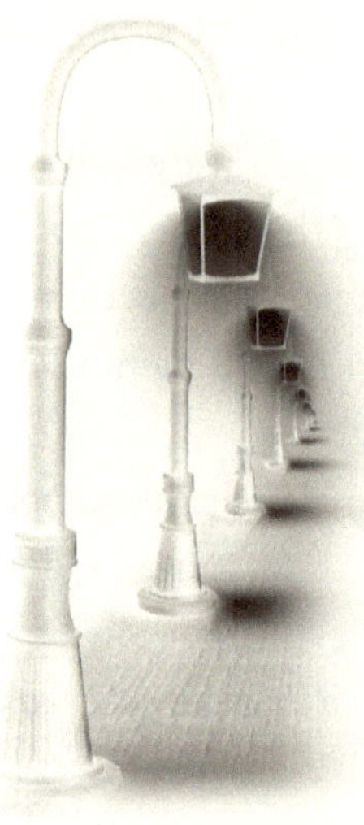

CHAPTER TWO

"You think Heidi was killed by a serial killer?" For a second, I let go of the steering wheel, until a dip in the road nearly slung my Volvo out of its lane.

We skidded, causing Eli to seek the oh-shit handle.

"Dammit," I mumbled and quickly corrected our trajectory. "What serial killer?"

Surely, the local newspaper would have reported a string of murders in huge headlines. Even in our town, where the concentration of kin was higher than in most places and unsuspecting humans were accustomed to unexplained displays of violence, a killing spree would have proven the perfect fodder for journalists.

"The director thinks I'm barking up the wrong telephone pole." Eli slammed the back of his head against the headrest. "There has been a number of seemingly unrelated murders. Like, a five-year-old troll boy drowned even though he was an excellent swimmer. A teenage satyr got killed in a hit-and-run. The fae matriarch's niece, thirteen, was shot, of all things."

That last death had made the news. "If they have nothing in common, how are they related?"

"First, they were all kin. Kids and teens of ten different races killed in ten different ways over the past few months. Seriously, not one over the age of twenty. Do you know the chances of that happening?"

"People die for all sorts of reasons and not all at the hands of a serial killer. Drowning sounds accidental to me."

"I'm not claiming one guy is responsible for all the deaths in Silverton, but we're not talking about fragile humans slipping in the bathroom here."

"Just don't put Heidi in the same pot with other victims."

"I'm not. I even thought the killer had hung up his killing tools because the last death happened more than three weeks ago. Fact is, though, these ten cases are probably the work of a single killer, and Heidi could be number eleven. It's not proof, but I'm telling you, something's fishy here."

Even without doing the math in my head, I knew he was on to something. The likelihood that different sources had spawned all these deaths was extremely low. Kin were resilient, with long lifespans. Werewolves alone could live for centuries.

"Let's assume you're right." I briefly peered at him. "Why would anyone kill them? You said yourself. They're kids."

"When we know the why, we'll know the who." He got out his cell and started typing. "Just give me a chance to prove it."

I turned the radio up and drove with my mouth locked, letting the buildings pass by in a blur. Had I made a huge mistake trusting Eli? I was a crime virgin, a newbie adventurer. If it was excitement I was after, I should have started with the mysterious case of Parker's missing sausage—which had sparked one hell of an atmosphere for a day—and not with Heidi's death. But no one had more at stake than me. I was the one who'd taken on responsibility for her.

Not that looking out for her had been easy. As she got older, she assimilated more into the pack, but her label as the 'baby' of the pack never left her. She used this to her advantage, even broke curfew a few times, confident I wouldn't get her into trouble with Parker. That's how sure she was of my affection for her. Maybe that meant I did a good enough job being her brother.

Until today.

The headquarters of the Interracial Enforcement Agency loomed over the West side like the watchful organization it was. Simple 'IEA' lettering in light-green, subtly lit, projected up from the roof. It blended seamlessly into the landscape of techy and financial institutions. Scores of trees dotted the spaces between the concrete, their leaves adding splotches of red and orange to the sea of gray.

I slowed the car and let my gaze scale the height of the building.

"What's up?" Eli asked.

"I've never been inside. We prefer to stay well clear of you lot."

"Yeah, why is that? We're good people."

I stopped at a traffic light and shot him a *you're kidding* look. "Not a fan."

"Okay, we're not all good people. I get it. To you, we're patsies of the seven kinlords that rule the seven most powerful races. And yes, they do set our agenda to an extent. But wouldn't you rather have us around than not? Someone has to keep kin in check. Better yet, wouldn't it be nice if we all got along?"

"You're asking me if I'd rather get a bullet in my *left* eye or in my *right* eye." I pressed the accelerator and headed toward the main entrance.

"Drive 'round the back. We have a body in our trunk, or have you forgotten?"

If only.

"All I'm saying is werewolves don't answer to the IEA." I kept my head straight to concentrate on the road, where the first raindrops pinged against my windshield. "There are no werewolves in Alethia, and we have no werewolf kinlord."

"Alethia was created to give all races a place free from humans, yet not even a single werewolf wanted to go? Don't get me wrong, I know it doesn't seem much of a paradise anymore, but it was designed to be a safe haven, all these centuries ago. And yet your kind stayed right here. Seems weird to me."

"Alethia is dark and has neither moon nor sun." I navigated the one-way streets in the vague hope of finding my way back to the IEA's building. "And although the moon has little influence over me now, it still dictates a werewolf's first few shifts."

"I didn't know that."

The heavens opened, and a torrent of rain gushed toward the ground, almost drowning out the noise from my engine.

"As you said, those poor bastards seeking a safe haven are all trapped now." I spoke louder and turned on the wipers. "At the mercy of monsters. Not so much the minor kinlords, but Lathan, the demon kinlord, and Mehmet, the vampire kinlord, have terrifying reputations."

"Fully deserved."

"Should they escape..."

"Mehmet tried." Eli shifted in his seat, perhaps discomforted by the actions of his kinlord. "Not long ago. We're still dealing with the fallout."

"Lathan tries to escape all the time." I drummed my thumb against the steering wheel. "He has a thing for Ivy. Before she and Parker got together, Lathan did some crazy shit to win her heart. Long story. Anyway, one day soon, he's going to succeed."

"Not while he and Mehmet are fighting each other." Eli laughed. "Here's to the continued animosity between kin."

"Says Mr. We-Should-All-Love-Each-Other."

"How about werewolves and vampires love each other, and to hell with the rest of them?"

'If wishes were rabbits, werewolves would feast,' as the old saying went. Of course, joining Eli in the hunt for a killer was already a stunning show of solidarity with the fang brigade. Especially with Parker's potential wrath breathing down my neck. Still, I'd made my decision.

"Vampires and werewolves united." A trickle of doubt hovered in my throat. "Sounds like a plan."

"Good news is, we're changing—slowly, but steadily. After Mehmet's attempt to seize control over our operations, more and more of our officers now demand independence from the kinlords. Ours should be an agency that caters to everyone."

We bounced down an uneven path, once or twice jostled against each other. He didn't seem to mind the contact. Nor did I. His scent titillated my nostrils, his voice was oddly melodious, yet neither seemed quite real. Nothing did tonight. Maybe the lateness of the hour played with my mind. It was one thirty at night—a little more than five hours before I'd have to report to Parker.

I finally located the unassuming gate, unmanned and with the bar up, and drove onto a small parking lot.

"Anyway, we werewolves do fine on our own." I'd upped the frostiness in my tone, even though letting my frustrations out on Eli was a dick move.

"You're in denial." He gave a close-lipped smile that lasted only a second. "I respect that."

"Denial my ass. About what?"

"I do a fair amount of traveling and hear things. Your pack has pissed off the other packs with the way you bulldoze over your rules and customs. You allowed a vampire and a demon into your pack. While the other packs scramble to achieve a level of power that rivals yours, you're becoming increasingly isolated. In other words, you're getting too big for your britches."

As if we didn't know. "How do you get your information?"

"I'm a friendly guy. When Florian isn't around stealing the limelight, people talk to me." His words carried bite.

Clearly, Florian was a sore spot for both of us.

My mother used to say love had nothing to do with life, and that I should find a nice Indonesian female and settle down. Putting aside Mother's blatant delusions about my sexuality, she had a point. Feelings tended to get in the way. Trouble was, loneliness quickly became a default position. It wasn't that I needed any*one* specifically in my life, but I needed something.

Maybe I should get a hobby, try something new.

"Do I park just anywhere?" I slowed and squinted past my hard-working wipers at the tall building. Visiting the IEA headquarters with a vampire by my side certainly was *new*.

"No one's here at this time, so park where you want." Eli gestured around the empty lot.

I slipped into the first space near the entrance and killed the headlights. While I unfastened the seat belt and climbed out, Eli had already rounded the car and opened the trunk.

He looked inside at Heidi's unmoving body. "She's so young."

I came up behind him, my throat too tight to speak.

"Are you okay?" he asked.

"I will be." Once we'd caught the killer, the whole pack would gather for the Mourning, and we'd run as wolves and howl for one half night, then feast and console each other for one half day. I just had to keep my shit together until then.

I reached in to scoop her into my arms, careful not to bang her head against the lid. Her body weighed nothing without that huge personality to inhabit it. Every week brought a new hair color, every day brought fresh drama. She'd had a mouth on her, for sure, and had sulking down pat. Occasionally, her veneer slipped, and she showed the innocence that never fully went away, but always, it lurked behind curse words, cynicism, and a pair of eyes that had seen far too much.

"Heidi came to us after her parents, both rogues, were killed by hunters looking for a good time." I blew a spot of lint off her forehead. "She was young then, five years old. A happy child, all things considered."

Eli closed the trunk just as a gust of wind tore at his hair. He didn't smooth it down, and it was a good thing my hands were already full, or I'd have done it for him.

"At least most of the time." I stepped aside to let him take the lead. "I never asked if she could remember watching her parents getting killed, but now and then, she'd get a far-away look, and her expression would shutter."

Eli stopped walking and turned, seemingly unconcerned by raindrops. "I'm sorry."

"Don't be sorry." My voice was gruff now, too full of feelings that had no outlet. "Just help me find the monster that did this."

"I promise."

His smile had vanished, hidden away by a closed expression of his own. Vampires were born out of pain. The pain of being torn out of their life, out of society. The pain that accompanied their hunger. Most of all, the pain they caused trying to still it.

Eli headed toward the glass door and held his eye close to a sensor. The lock disengaged with a click, and he pulled out the door to let me enter.

Inside, there was no welcome mat on which to wipe my feet, and I had no choice but to add my wet boot prints to Eli's. A brightly lit corridor snaked around one corner and another, all the way to a sturdy door. A sign identified the room behind it as the morgue.

I stopped short, sudden enough for my boot to give a squeak. The morgue was where dead people went. The minute we'd step inside the room, Heidi would be one of them, for real.

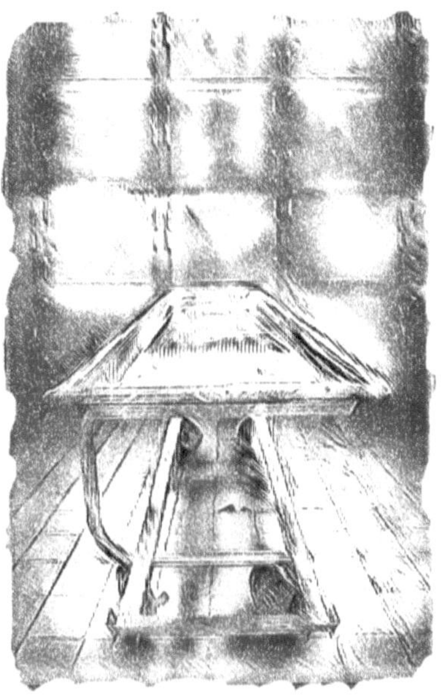

Eli slid his arm past my waist and twisted the doorknob. The lights came on by themselves. With the utmost care, he nudged me toward a shiny table under a globe-shaped lamp. The scent of death I'd expected wasn't the one that hit me. Rather, a chemical explosion took place in my nostrils. Instruments were laid out in parallel alignment on a draped cloth, and a deep sink by the wall sparkled under the lights. Even the floor was polished to a high shine.

I placed Heidi on top of the table and propped my hands next to her. "This surface is cold. The whole room is."

"She's not feeling it." Eli's palm found the back of my neck and held tight.

None of the wolves would have touched me in this moment. Werewolf kin sought comfort from each other, found refuge in each other's embrace, but it was the pack's choice not to include me in this. Not that I blamed them. I was the second in command, and it was my job to tear them a new one if they stepped out of line. In fact, Florian had been the first person in a long time to pat my back or place his arm on my shoulder.

I closed my eyes for a few seconds. Eli's skin wasn't warm, not really. Still, the weight of his hand was enough to ground me.

"We need to find out where Heidi was when she was poisoned." His smooth voice glided across my skin, unscathed by the harsh content of his words.

"And who left her outside our door and why." I ran my fingers, once again, through her purple hair. Even damp it was coarse like straw from too much dyeing. Every week, she reinvented herself.

"What's wrong?" Eli asked, firming his touch.

"Just wondering what I could have done differently." Her jacket and top had ridden up to her waist, and I smoothed both down.

My fingertips were like icicles. They had been cold the day I met Heidi, too. Her palm had been sticky from jelly candy she'd been eating, or rather, licking out of her tiny fist, but her grip had been strong. Those big blue eyes had latched on to *me*, of all people, and hadn't let go. I saw my reflection in them, right next to her grief and her need for love. She'd known nothing of race and sexuality, of the quirks that made up our personalities and attracted or repulsed others. That look in her eyes, that longing for family— that was a language I understood.

"This isn't your fault." Eli pressed closer against me, and his breath grazed my ear, teasing the wolf inside. "We can't watch them twenty-four-seven."

"I need to get back home." I twisted away from the metal table and from his proximity. "We have cameras on our property. They should have caught whoever dropped her off."

Why hadn't I thought of this earlier? The sight of one body shouldn't have made me this careless. I wasn't that delicate.

"You wolves have a Cloud account?" Eli asked.

"Yeah."

The barricade of square metal doors in front of me might be hiding corpses, but *they* evoked no pity in me. No, when it came to strangers, I was as steel-hearted as I'd always suspected.

Eli nudged me. "You know the password?"

I blinked hard to help me turn my focus away from the wall of death. "What?"

"Do you know the password to your Cloud account?"

"No. Why?"

"Never mind. I've called in Clarence. Excellent hacker. He's a troll." Eli mimicked a sizeable stomach. "Anyway, put him in front of a computer, and he'll get into any account without alerting anyone."

"I'm not letting you hack into our account, dude." I crisscrossed my arms. "If you think that's even on the cards, you're tripping."

"You should look up the definition of hacking." Eli raised his eyebrows in an exaggerated lift. "Cheer up. I promise, if you don't tell Parker, I won't, and then he has no reason to get angry, right?"

Parker was going to be pissed about my cooperation with the IEA already, but this wasn't about him or me. This night was about Heidi and the asshole who'd killed her.

"Clearly, I can't stop you." A heavy scowl emphasized my objection.

"Now you're getting it." Eli leaned in close. "Don't give up on me. I know what I'm doing."

He was more than a pretty face, no doubt. For now, I'd follow his lead, but this room, this place of death, didn't help us. Heidi's killer was out there, and the sooner we got back on the streets, the better.

I marched to the door with my chin up. "Waiting for an invitation?"

My neck felt naked without his touch, but my head already buzzed from here till Christmas, and I didn't need any more conflicting emotions.

"Give me a moment." Eli pressed his cell to his ear. His instructions to whoever was on the other end of the line were to the point.

There was a chance that partnering up with him had been a good move and not just the action of someone too distraught to think clearly. He had the resources and smarts to guide me to the killer. Unfortunately, the one thing neither of us could control was the luck needed to get us to that point by seven o'clock.

Jeez, how many times had I told our wolves not to go Lone Ranger on us? How many asses had I busted for leaving by the back door for dates without getting approval first? I was one crappy role model tonight.

"Clarence says he's already on his way." Eli pocketed his phone. "He'll be here in five."

With my future in the balance, five minutes seemed like an eternity. Yet I nodded and looked back at Heidi. Gripped the door handle. Didn't turn it.

Eli came up from behind and touched my arm. "She's safe here."

He was more tactile than his brother, but as much as a comforting hand was what I *wanted*, a steady mind was what I *needed*.

"It doesn't feel right to leave her." I gave a grim chuckle. "Isn't *that* a stupid thing to say?"

"Nothing about this is right." Eli squeezed my arm for a few seconds. "I've already texted Mina, the medical examiner. She'll be here soon."

"No autopsy. You promised."

"She'll take blood and will check Heidi's body for clues. Nothing else. More importantly, she'll keep Heidi company." He slapped my back. "Come on, dude. Let's find the bastard who did this."

What twist had my life taken for me to trust another vampire?

Parker was my alpha, and justice was his to seek and to

dispense. My actions would probably get me demoted, but if he even suspected Eli ensured my help not just with his words but with a killer smile, worse would follow.

I turned the knob and left the room, head held high, safe in the knowledge I was monumentally screwed.

CHAPTER THREE

The IT department, as Eli had called it, consisted of three desks, six monitors, and too much paper for a group of people who worshipped the digital world. The pervading scent of ink only reinforced the contradiction. Torn posters reminding computer users not to open email attachments from unknown sources should have been unnecessary, but maybe even the IEA had procedures to follow.

Clarence, the hacker, looked like any white human male and blended in with the world undetected like the rest of us kin, but his generous stomach and overall size told their own story to those in the know. He was a troll, from his worn shoes to his creased blue shirt.

Eli stood between Clarence and me, using our chair backs as supports for his elbows. Now and again, he pointed at the screen or asked a question, but mostly, he quietly hummed to himself.

"What's going on?" a deep voice thundered from the door.

"Director Vanguard." Eli moved enough to allow me a glance over my shoulder.

"I asked you a question, Dupree." The hulk of a man with skin only a few shades darker than mine slammed the door.

He was wrapped head to boots in a see-through plastic rain protector, which he took off and shook out. Clarence used his upper body to shield his keyboard against the flying raindrops, while the beige carpet absorbed most of the load.

Eli straightened with a quiet sigh. The dangerous kind. "Following my hunch about the serial killer."

"How many times? The serial killer lives in your mind. Why don't—" The director fixed me with his gaze. "A werewolf? You brought a werewolf to the office? Are you out of your mind?"

The only way he could have pegged me as a werewolf was if he'd kept tabs on our pack. But then, he was the director of the IEA. He probably had a live feed streamed to his office, covering all the kin in Silverton.

"My sanity is an area you should definitely explore." If Eli had been chewing bubblegum, he'd be popping it in the director's face, for sure. "As for me, I have work to do."

"You're untouchable for now, but that's going to change." The director glowered at Eli. "Neither of you is up to solving a crossword, let alone a serial killer case even if there was one, which there isn't. You're not an alpha." He focused on me. "And Dupree isn't the hotshot his brother is. Just my luck I ended up with the wrong family member."

Eli stilled, his body and face rigid.

Vanguard's light blue shirt and black chinos gave him a respectable appearance, but I knew his type. He was a bully. I shoved my chair back and got to my feet. If nothing else, my wide build made me look as dangerous as Eli actually was.

"I'm not going to schmutz up your office with werewolf juice, so back off." I leaned my head to the side. "Although I find your threat odd. If Eli's gut pays off, it's a win for your agency. If not, you can use his failure against him."

Eli and I had a couple of inches on him, although I hoped it was my diplomacy that finally led to him storming out of the room.

"Standing up to the director takes balls." Eli slapped my back.

"Lucky I have two of them. Besides, next to Parker, your director is a teddy bear. Still, a heads-up would have been nice. I didn't think your boss would be here at two in the morning."

"Neither did I. Don't worry about him, though. He thinks I'm a trouble maker because I don't always color within the lines. It offends his sense of order. He's a stickler for hierarchy. But if he had the power to kick me out, he'd have done it ages ago."

We stood, each with our arms crossed, while Clarence typed away furiously on his keyboard.

"How come you were dressed in the middle of the night anyway?" Eli lifted his head. "Thought you lot went to bed early."

"Yeah, but we had a party a couple of nights ago." I suppressed a snort. "I was catching up on work. But early or late, I'm not going to walk around the house in PJs or boxers."

"Ah, I'm a boxer man myself."

"TMI, Eli." I raised my eyebrows. "Way too much."

"There's nothing wrong with boxers." His gaze was fully on me. "Besides, it's your home."

"One I share with about twenty other people." I stared at the back of Clarence's head, but even with my face aimed away from Eli, I felt his focus on me no less than I would the firm touch of a hand. "I wasn't raised to be casual about these things."

Rollo, our pack's enforcer, often wore shorts around the house and more than once, he'd made himself a sandwich dressed in nothing other than boxers and a T-shirt, but my position was associated with a certain etiquette.

"Some are raised with a silver spoon in their mouth, others with a stick up their ass." Eli didn't grin as much as curled up his upper lip to show his perfect teeth. "You're grown up now, so if you want to walk around in boxers or even naked, go for it. Your friends might appreciate it."

"As if I don't stick out already."

"You stick out?" He laughed. "Hate to burst your bubble, dude, but you're the stereotypical furball."

"Says the stereotypical fang boy."

His pale skin and good looks were one hundred percent vampire romance novel, although he had a swagger and an intensity that promised violence rather than sparkles.

"What's a typical furball, anyway?" I asked.

"Furballs are stick-up-your-ass-ish. Superior, maybe a little smug. Proper, you know."

"On the outside, maybe." I moved us to the other side of the room so poor Clarence didn't have to referee between us. "We can be fun."

"Sure, but do you ever do anything spontaneous?" His voice was smooth enough, but his words made me edgy as hell.

"We throw a lot of parties. Pack-only. Sorry."

"Doesn't count. Do you ever go to a bar in the middle of the week?"

He and I led very different lives. "Not if I have to work the next morning."

"Fuck." He gave an unrestrained sigh. "I got to you in the nick of time then. The night's young, and I have a corrupting influence."

He winked, and this time it wasn't a trick of the light.

Florian told me that Eli had once asked out Ivy, long before she hooked up with Parker, so I'd assumed Eli was straight. But what if he liked men? Stranger things had happened.

Great, five hours until my personal doom, and here I was looking to get myself into worse trouble by falling for another vampire who, on top of that, thought me a snob.

"No time for play." My pitch dipped halfway through the sentence. "Heidi was important to me. She's why I'm here."

And she was the *only* reason.

"I promise, I didn't mean to make fun of you." He placed a hand on my shoulder and sought my gaze. "I know you're not a bore. You had a good time at Florian's bonding ceremony, didn't you? Even took part in the conga, if memory serves."

His attention didn't wander from my face, not to check on Clarence's progress, and certainly not to give me time to adjust to his proximity.

"I did." Even though my muscles tensed and I strained to appear normal, my breathing sped up.

He'd noticed me that night.

"I remember it well," he said. "Not least because of the puppy dog eyes you made over losing the love of your life."

The scent of wet leather coming from his jacket didn't do my concentration any favors.

"Hardly." My gaze went to the small window to my left, one miniscule flick to collect myself, and then back to him. "I was once attracted to Florian, and our link amplified those feelings, certainly. But from the beginning, it was us trying to make the best of the situation. Don't read too much into it."

"Anyway. Sorry we didn't get a chance to talk." He licked his lips, and I couldn't take my eyes off his mouth. "Maybe at the next party—"

"Guys?" Clarence shouted. "I'm in."

Eli turned. In an instant, Eli's touch was gone and so was the relative stillness of my mind. Shit. My internal compass was off. South was up, North was to the right, and East and West couldn't decide on a location. Slowly, though, I caught up with Clarence's words.

"There he is. Hang on." Clarence pressed a few keys on his keyboard. A device on the other side of the room whirred.

"Nicely done." I approached the screen, which showed the folders in the pack's Cloud account. "Do you have software here like the FBI? Facial recognition, that kind of stuff?"

"Kind of." Eli crossed the room to the noisy printer that coughed once before falling silent. He picked up two sheets and handed me one. "It's called legwork."

Always with the jokes. A defense mechanism that ran in his family, which begged the question, what emotions was *he* hiding?

The guy in the picture had an almost shaven head, not bad looking, with maybe an Italian or Hispanic background. He was climbing the stairs leading to my pack's door, with Heidi in his arms.

So, that's what a killer looked like.

"We don't get much funding," Eli said. "As you can imagine, the people we police don't like giving money for the privilege, and the kinlords only shell out in return for specific requests. Favors, you know." He tapped the side of his nose, and then slapped Clarence's shoulder. "Thanks, dude. Stick around for a while, okay?"

Clarence gave a casual salute. "Aye, my Capitan."

Our mini-breakthrough hadn't come a minute too soon. For the first time, my future didn't appear that bleak anymore. Still, it would be premature to get carried away. We only had the killer's face, and we still had to find him. For all we knew, he could have hightailed it out of Silverton the minute he'd dropped off Heidi.

"Come on. There's a guy who I think can help us." Eli pointed at the photo on the sheet in his hand. "Unless you've seen the dude before?"

I studied the slightly grainy photo of the killer again. Where were the tears he should be shedding over his actions? The guilt, or even the terror? That bastard was placing the body of a werewolf at the doorstep of an entire pack. Each one of us would have torn him apart on the spot if we'd known. But this guy? He looked as calm as a courier dropping off a package.

"No idea who that is." My grim smile drew malice entirely from my pounding heart. "But I can't wait to make his acquaintance."

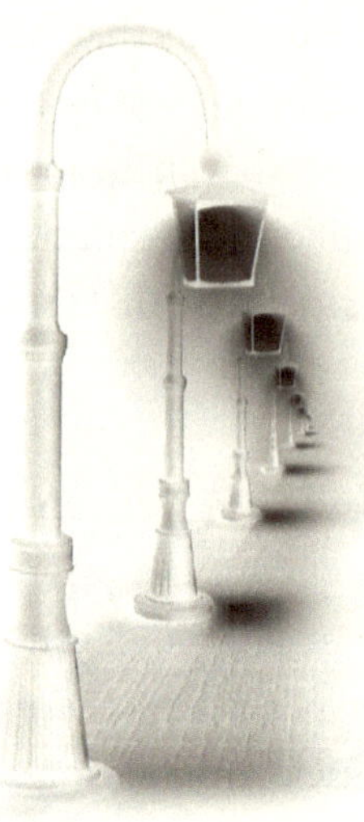

CHAPTER FOUR

I rolled into a spot outside a greenish building. Thunder rumbled, followed five Mississippi-seconds later by lightning that illuminated the sky. Darkness returned quickly, save for the streetlights that reflected over and over in the puddles. We got out of the car and dashed down a narrow alley that led past one building, with water splashing up my pants and soaking my socks.

Starting our mission with wet feet didn't bode well.

A set of stairs led up to a white door. We crowded under the roofed entrance, where it was dry, and Eli knocked.

"What can you tell me about this guy?" I all but huddled against him to escape stray raindrops.

"Name's Jack Gdansk." Eli stayed in place, allowing me a prime view of his light-blue eyes. "He's one of the agency's best informants. Low-level demon. A kind of middleman for the scum that hides deep in Silverton's underbelly. He's come through for us many times. Gotta warn you though, he's a character."

Eli knocked again, louder now.

"What was your thing with Director Vanguard about? He really can't stand you." I rolled my hands into fists inside my sleeves, if only to hide my impatience. If Eli's informant wasn't at home, did he have a plan B?

"Vanguard trained me and encouraged me, at least at the start." Eli leaned to the side to catch a view through a curtained window. "But recently he got his panties in a twist because my grand-sire demanded my promotion. Guess he feels threatened by me."

"How would your grand-sire pull that off?"

"My grand-sire is Mehmet, the vampire kinlord." He scoffed. "Lucky me, huh?"

"Your grand-sire is a kinlord? How did I not know that?"

"Not something any of us, especially my brother, is proud of. And as terrifying as his reputation is, the old man's a family guy, and he has a soft spot for us."

"Nepotism in the vampire world. Nice." I gave him a thumbs-up. "But I don't get it. Mehmet's a kinlord in Alethia. How can he wield such influence here?"

"You gotta understand the history." Eli held his face against the door lock and used both hands to shield his sight against extraneous light. "This goes back to the time before Alethia was created, when the kinlords ruled their subjects with an iron fist. Bonds were forged, relationships honed."

"It's my understanding that kinlords can't leave Alethia because the magic that keeps the realms apart repels their powers with equal and opposite force."

"True enough, but their minions, whose powers are negligible by comparison, often find ways to travel across." He aimed his gaze back at me for a few seconds. "They smuggle artefacts that extend the kinlords' reach across realms, they act as enforcers, strengthen old oaths, collect on ancient promises, and they run businesses in their kinlords' names. If you defy your kinlord, you're as good as dead."

"Even the satyrs or fae?"

"They're more lenient. Mehmet's bad enough, but Lathan's the worst by far. Without Mehmet, Lathan would have overthrown the minor kinlords a long time ago. He'd be unstoppable then."

I wouldn't want to go up against either.

"Jack," Eli shouted and smacked his palm repeatedly against the door. "Get your ass out of bed and open up."

The man who finally answered the door was a small, anxious fellow, with a penetrating stare. The kind you'd suspect of being high, but probably wasn't. His eyes were close together or maybe his face was too wide for his eyes; either way, he reminded me of a panda, an impression reinforced by his white shirt and the black pants he was just buttoning up.

"Eli." The guy hugged the much taller vampire. "What's going on?"

"Finally." Eli pushed the dude away with a hand. "Say hi to Ali."

The man rubbed his red nose while ogling me. A few seconds later, he waved Eli closer and leaned in. "He's a werewolf. Second to the pack's alpha."

"He knows," Eli whispered back. Then, with a normal voice, he added, "He's one of the good guys."

"In that case, come here." Jack hugged me close, pressing his ear against my shoulder.

My dripping wet clothes didn't dent his enthusiasm as his arms snaked to encircle me.

I stiffened.

In the end, it was Eli who pulled him off me by his collar.

"You shouldn't dry-hump every guy you meet." Eli deposited him back by the door.

"Not nice." Jack folded his arms. "I thought we were friends."

"That depends on whether you can help us." Eli unfolded the sheet from his pocket and handed it to him. "Seen him before?"

"Oh, I can't stay mad at you, pretty boy." Jack held the picture into the light coming from inside his apartment. "Hmm. You, your friend, and him? We should double date, the four of us."

"That guy's a murderer." I slid a finger across my throat to ram the news home.

"With a face like that?" Jack pressed his hand against his ribs. "Yeah, I know him. Doesn't look like you'd expect a killer to look, though."

"Where can we find him?" Eli stowed the picture away again.

"If I tell you, can I come?" Jack's eyes didn't flash, but his roguish expression almost demanded it. "Please? I've never been on official IEA business before." His smile vanished as he focused on me. "I've always wanted to be an agent or a cop, but the knee, you know." He bent low to grip his leg.

In some way, he reminded me of Heidi. Like her, he believed the greatest unfairness on the planet was that it didn't revolve around him.

"No, you can't come." Eli shifted and looked taller. "Who is he?"

Jack fell back against his doorframe and pushed out his bottom lip. "Rude. I'm not telling you."

"I. Need. A. Name." Eli prodded Jack's ribcage with every syllable. "Now."

Jack made a farting noise with his mouth.

Eli's hand curled and his eyes narrowed.

Despite the fact that Jack's age was north of twenty-five even if he'd been human, his tantrum merely copied the performance Heidi would have given in his position. Jack could draw this out forever.

"I'm on a clock." I nudged Eli. "Let him show us where to find the guy, for crying out loud."

The name of the murderer alone wouldn't do the pack any good in coming to terms with Heidi's death. I needed to serve up the killer in person. Before Parker woke. Or Heidi wouldn't be my only loss today.

Eli kept the tension in his body for another second, then dropped his shoulders. "Fine."

"Yes! Oh man, oh man." Jack ran inside. "Just a second."

"You sure about that?" Although Eli's hood was drawn deep over his face, it didn't obscure his squint.

Werewolves had rules, and although not all of us followed them all the time, I did. It was what made me reliable, a calm oak Parker could lean on, no matter the storm. Tonight, though, rules didn't exist. Only my mission did.

"Parker's going to chew me up either way for my unsanctioned excursion, for sure, but if I don't have anything to show for it in the morning, the consequences will be ten times worse." I tapped the photo. "I want the killer, and I want him before Parker gets up."

"When we find the killer, we're taking him to our HQ for interrogation first." Eli lifted his hood to catch my gaze. "You know that, right?"

I glowered. "The killer's ass belongs to the pack."

"This guy may have killed more people than Heidi. Other families want answers, too. Is this all about revenge for you, or about justice?"

"Let's go, guys." Jack returned and wrapped one hand around his upper arm to highlight guns he didn't have. "The three Muscleteers to the rescue."

Neither Eli nor I laughed. With the disagreement still hanging between us, we rushed back to the street.

Inside my Volvo, I slid my hood off my head and turned on the ignition. The air from the vents dried my face, but it would take more than that to get rid of the confining stiffness of my pants. Eli's demand hadn't even been that unreasonable, but an IEA interrogation would be pointless. The pack would get what we needed out of the killer, one way or another. Werewolves were damn good at that.

If I had to cross Eli to get my way, then that was a price worth paying.

Yet for now, we had to postpone resolving our difference of opinion, because, first, we had to find the guy.

Jack, meanwhile, had made himself at home in the backseat. He'd constructed a small pile out of his backpack and jacket that looked too formal for a guy that hyper.

Leaning forward, he held onto my headrest and breathed his directions into my ear.

I took the road back into town, past the cafés and restaurants, to where tall buildings sliced the sky. The wipers worked fast, dealing with the rain we desperately needed after the dry spell, but despite their efforts, the illumination from streetlamps and traffic lights smeared into blinding stars.

A flash of lightning projected abstract patterns into the darkness. Heidi hated this kind of weather. As a kid, when thunder got too loud or lightning too frequent, she'd climb into my bed. For *my* safety, of course.

"Isn't Eli awesome?" Jack met my gaze in the rearview mirror. "He might only be the assistant director, but he's destined for great things."

"You're smitten, aren't you?" I accelerated despite the dangerous conditions. We'd already wasted too much time.

"I've asked him out many times. Guess I'm not his type." Jack's head popped through the space between the two headrests to breathe on Eli for a change. "Is Ali your type? He's also an assistant, in a way. An assistant to his alpha. You must have a lot in common."

I pressed my lips together against the rising stream of denial that wanted out. Eli was easy on the eye, but my dirty laundry was mine, and mine alone.

"Maybe he simply doesn't swing that way." I pushed back Jack's head without taking my eyes off the street. "It's a shocking fact of life, but not everyone in California is gay."

"I can tell, the same way I can tell with you." Jack's voice was a tight ball of self-satisfaction. "I study people, see. That's my hobby. What makes them tick? Who do they like? Being observant helps me stay alive."

Was that code for blackmail? Next time I should ask more questions before working with IEA informants.

"I know for a fact Eli once asked out a girl." I kept any reproach out of my tone. Eli was a single guy, free to date who he wanted.

"I did?" Eli turned to look at me. "Who?"

"Ivy," I said with the same coolness.

"Christ, I once asked her to a bar so we could talk because she's tight with Florian. Did my brother tell you it was more than that?"

"He might have." I shifted into a more comfortable position and slowed for the red lights up ahead. "Not that it's any of my business. And she's pretty awesome."

"Don't listen to Florian. He doesn't know me." Eli quietly cleared his throat. "If he did, he'd have told you I'm more into dark, brown eyes."

Heat cascaded through my body. For a second, I allowed myself to wonder if my dark brown eyes qualified.

"If you and Eli don't hit it off, I'm single." Jack kicked my seat. "Maybe we could catch a movie?"

I fixated him with my gaze via the rearview mirror. "Let's focus on finding the guy in the photo, all right?"

"Okay." Jack gave a sigh of the XXL variety. "Man, you're just as cold as Eli."

As if he ever stood a chance with the vampire anyway. Eli could have his pick of guys or girls, although I didn't exactly hate that he swung for my team.

I took in the neon lights of the clubs and bars that lined the sidewalk. Their reflections multiplied in the rain-kissed streets. At night, anybody could be whoever they wanted to be. I could be a guy Eli might fall for, or someone who caught a killer. The morning's sun would chase away the hiding places, though. Would I be a hero, or simply a pathetic werewolf who'd gambled away his security and social standing?

"Here. Stop here." Jack's finger shot forward. "See that building? It has a bar on the top two levels. You'll find Max here."

The corner building he pointed at stood around ten or twelve stories high. A handful of windows were lit, including the large lobby, and an orange glow enveloped the top of the building.

"Max who?" I threaded into a parking spot and turned off the engine.

"Hoffmann. The dude in the photo. Not a nice guy, by the way."

"What's he into?" I asked.

"Anything you need him to do. Robbery. Assault. They say he can dislocate a knee cap with one hundred percent accuracy on the first kick." Jack kept his chipper tone.

"What makes you think he's here at this time?" Eli pointed at the Volvo's clock, which showed two fifty-five.

"He's a sandman," Jack said. "You know, sleeps during the day, parties at night? This is his favorite hangout."

"Sandman men, sandmans, whatever you call them, they're usually peaceful, aren't they?" Eli slowly undid his seatbelt. "What is he doing killing people?"

I waited for a car to pass us, then pushed open the door. The sandman would answer all our questions soon enough.

"Maybe he's diversifying." Jack shrugged. "You got to in today's climate."

Eli climbed out of the car and leaned back to take in the entire building.

"Hang on." Jack placed his foot onto the sidewalk. "I'm coming."

"No way." Eli pushed the demon informant back into the Volvo and slammed the door shut. "As if."

Jack rolled down his window. "We had a deal."

With rain spraying my face, I joined Eli on the sidewalk and wiped my eyes. So far, Jack had seen my indulgent side. Time for tough love.

"You can stay in the car or walk home." I indicated back the way we came. "Take it or leave it."

"Fine." Jack fell back into his seat. "I'll stay."

Tough love for the win.

Eli and I sprinted to the glass doors of the building and entered. I thoroughly wiped my shoes on the large mat before drying my face with a tissue.

"Seriously, dude?" Eli gave half an eyeroll.

"Whatever." I tucked the tissue away and made a beeline for the elevators.

The harsh lights overhead blatantly refused to accept the late hour and simulated an atmosphere brighter than daylight. The black boards behind the reception tracked eight stories of lawyers, accountants, and financial consultants.

"Have a nice evening," a man wearing a red jacket and a bowtie called after us.

Eli gave a half-baked wave as we hurried past his desk.

"You go up to the top floor. To make sure we don't miss him, I'll take the stairs to the one below." He crossed his arms. "I want to talk to this Hoffmann guy. Please don't go rogue on me."

"Why? What do you care, as long as we get justice?"

"Because..." Eli swept his gaze over the silver doors of the elevator and then back to me. "The director thinks I don't deserve my position. He's wrong. I might not be good at much, but I'm good at my job."

Who would possibly doubt him? Every step of the way, he'd had answers. What did it matter whether Vanguard slapped his back at the end of the investigation? The director was a jerk. Still, something told me Eli's need for recognition wasn't about vanity. It was about acceptance. Sure, getting justice for Heidi was my priority, but being the one who found the killer... For once, my pack would see me not as the reliable stickler who became Parker's second in command through friendship, but as a guy who rose through the ranks on merit.

"I get it." I shrugged. "But after that, he's mine."

"Deal. And thank you."

I pushed the button. "You're welcome."

Eli shuffled next to me for a second before hurrying to a door marked *private*. Vampire speed was legendary, and he'd probably reach his destination before the elevator had made its way down to me.

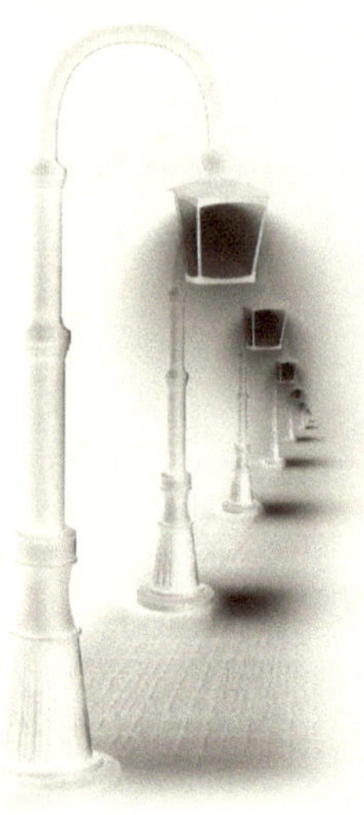

CHAPTER FIVE

T he metal doors opened, and I pressed the button to the top level. My hands were stiff, my senses alert.

Two months ago, I'd suggested manning our security room twenty-four seven rather than the spot-checks we executed now. If Parker had heeded my advice, the killer wouldn't have gotten away. He'd have been detained the second he set foot on our estate.

Heidi would still be dead, but at least my fist would be buried in someone's face now rather than balled up, waiting.

Never mind the would-haves and maybes, though. If the killer was here, I'd find him. If he ran, I'd catch him. Either way, his ass was going to be mine.

I entered a softly lit rooftop bar that was more lounge than dive. The inside serving area was protected from the elements by panoramic windows that revealed a three-hundred-and-sixty-degree terrace. Outside, black leather couches, oversized lamps, and fire pits vied for attention, while the glass walls that surrounded the seating areas offered a clear view of the Silverton skyline.

Rain and lightning had caused the twenty or so men and women to sit inside, where jazz music weaved between tall plants and wine glasses. The owners had worked hard to create a nostalgic atmosphere, and if Bugsy Malone and his moll had busted in, I wouldn't have batted an eyelid. I walked in a large circle, along the fruit-scented bottles lining the area behind the counter, to the corner where the newly-in-love had gathered, and back to a piano tucked into a corner.

Heidi's killer sat sandwiched between a wall and a small table. His slim frame almost blended into the shadow of a palm tree as he nursed a beer with the same handsome face as in the picture. By the time I was done with this guy, his mother wouldn't want to look at him.

Why wasn't the bastard at home, washing Heidi's death from his skin? Or at church, confessing his sins?

I rolled my neck and advanced toward the table.

His gaze snapped up, and his expression froze.

A growl erupted in my throat, and I leaned in. "I've been looking for you, Max."

"Oh fuck. You're one of them." His wide eyes appeared glazed, and the ribbon of beer breath told its own story. "I knew the werewolf girl was a mistake. I just fucking knew it."

His gaze darted, but there was nowhere to go. I grabbed him by the collar of his dark jacket and yanked him to his feet.

"For what it's worth, I'm sorry they had to die." He didn't even raise a hand in defense. "And your girl, she was nice. Wicked sense of humor. Really."

Many people lied all day long, either because they hoped it would benefit them or simply for humorous purposes. Accordingly, some falsehoods stank more than others. Not a whiff of a lie came from the killer.

No doubt that wouldn't last.

"Then why did you kill her?" I shoved Hoffmann into the wall and closed my hand around his neck. The animal inside wanted to do much, much worse to him, and it took willpower to remain in human form.

"You wouldn't understand," he wheezed.

"She was too young to die. Too good to die." I tightened my grip. "You worthless piece of shit."

Hoffmann was going to feel the pain his victims had felt. I squeezed harder by the second, watched his face turn red. He hadn't just killed a young werewolf girl under my care, he had extinguished a flame that burned more brightly than any I'd encountered.

A hand dragged me back by my shoulder.

I spun and bared my teeth. "Don't, Eli. Just don't."

"Take a breath." Eli increased the pressure on my shoulder blade and held on until I'd let go of the sandman. "There. That's good."

I jerked out of Eli's grasp and planted my fist in the wall, where it left a jagged hole. My knuckles barely registered the pain.

"Max Hoffmann?" Eli flashed his badge. "IEA. Your ass is mine."

I leaned against the broken wall, reining in my breathing, focusing my rage into a spot. Heidi's killer was caught, so where was the jubilation? The satisfaction? Instead, memories of the little girl I knew mingled with hallucinations of the woman she'd have become. Together, the images played tricks on my mind, wove cobwebs in my brain and blew them right up again. Worse, though, were the floods of panic that forced their way through my lungs. Like watching a shark documentary and suddenly remembering I'd been holding my breath.

Spirits, if you hear me, take care of my Heidi.

A man in the bar's black-and-white uniform entered our corner but speedily booked it out of here. Tomorrow or later in the week, I'd send them a check to cover the damage I'd caused. Heidi's death wasn't their fault.

"Fine. You got me." The sandman held out his hands for cuffing. "At least it's over, you know?"

"Come on then." Eli grabbed his collar instead. "We have many questions."

"Hey, you got him." Jack appeared behind Eli and twisted his mouth into a grim line. "There's no escaping now, Max. These two are going to beat the confession out of you, and I'll be watching every step of the way."

Max started and drew a sharp breath. "But I didn't—"

"Don't lie." I punched him. "We have you on camera."

His jaw ripped to the side with a crunch that wasn't loud enough.

"Whoa," Jack shouted. "That must have hurt."

"Shut up." Eli glowered at the demon before skewering me with a reproachful look. "And you, stop punching the killer. There'll be time for that later."

I wasn't a four-year-old pup to be told off in this fashion, but any comment to that effect wouldn't have helped my position. Not when Eli was right.

Hoffmann coiled to the side.

Damn. His lightning-fast movement startled me into stepping back.

He twisted out from under Eli's arm and sprinted away. By the time I'd reached out to grab him, he was already approaching the rooftop's glass doors.

Eli and I set off to run after our killer.

"He's getting away!" Jack rushed ahead of us.

Eli collided with Jack and stumbled. "Fuck." His legs folded away from under him.

I swerved around their tumbling shapes and followed the sandman out onto the terrace, where puddles splashed up my already wet pant legs. Hoffmann zigzagged past the tables, as if looking for a way off the roof, and then stopped at the glass railing.

"Don't come closer." He swung one leg over the see-through barrier. His voice didn't just shake. It rattled. "I'll jump."

The rain-washed darkness filled my sensitive nose with earthy scents and my lungs with the stench of car fuel, even all the way up here. Heidi had loved the smell of fuel. It filled her mind with adventure, she'd once told me.

"We just want to talk." I stopped about twenty feet from him, slowing my movements. "Okay?"

His gaze flitted wildly across the roof before finally settling back on me. "Talk? You're suddenly interested in what I have to say?"

My punch to his jaw had clearly scared the bejesus out of him.

"Sure." I regulated my tone to a level pitch. "Just talk."

Fast paces behind me gave little warning when Eli grabbed my arm to brake his run.

"Stay cool, man." Eli raised his hands but kept his distance. "Don't do it."

Lightning split the night, illuminating Hoffmann's short dark hair.

"You're the IEA, right? You gotta protect me." Hoffmann's gaze latched on to Eli's. "I'll tell you everything, but you protect me. Deal?"

"I can do that." Eli pushed in front of me. "You'll be safe. I promise."

Hoffmann's frame slacked, and a serene smile slightly parted his lips.

"Come on. Easy now." Eli had thrown his vampiric glamour over Hoffmann, and it was working.

Florian had once glamoured me—at my request—and I'd spilled secrets and clucked like a chicken with the lightest, happiest of feelings.

The sandman wasn't faring any better. He swayed toward us, and I ran to catch him. He used my shoulder as a crutch and slid toward safety, then I tugged on him to get his dangling leg back onto the rooftop, too.

"I'm sorry," Hoffmann murmured. His dazed eyes remained focused on Eli, and he straightened his back to stand unaided.

I shot Eli a grateful nod and gave the sandman some breathing space.

My temper, and Jack's encouragement, had nearly cost us the chance to discover what sick thoughts had driven Hoffmann to take a life that hadn't been fully lived yet. Eli had saved the day. Without his skills and intervention, we might have spent the rest of the night scraping Hoffmann's brain off the street.

"Oh shit." A waiter came running from inside the bar, carrying a bottle and two wine glasses in his hand. "Want me to call the police?"

"It's okay." Jack, who appeared behind the man, nudged him back by the sleeve of his black jacket. "They have the situation under control."

"Please don't touch me, sir." The waiter looked at the demon as if he was dirt.

Admittedly, Jack's attire wasn't quite what this place was accustomed to, but then neither was mine nor Eli's.

"Listen to me." Jack frowned and yanked the guy toward the glass doors. "Get out of here, I said."

The waiter shook off Jack's grip with force—and dropped the glasses. Both smashed into smithereens.

Eli glanced over his shoulder. "Will you shut the fuck up?"

"Wha—" Hoffmann blinked hard. "No. Please."

"Take it easy." I wrapped my hand around his arm again, even though the wet polyester of his sleeve didn't allow for a solid grip. "I got you."

"No. Please." He flailed his arms and leaned back to wrench his frame away.

"Come on. Work with me." I shifted my hand to his collar and tightened my hold.

He finally stilled, so much so a heavy raindrop perched on the end of his eyelashes. Blue eyes, so often associated with innocence, stared past my shoulder. A pained expression crossed his face.

Then he violently shoved me away.

I grabbed for him again and—

My hand closed around nothing. Hoffmann was already falling.

CHAPTER SIX

I continued to reach into thin air, but there was no do-over. As Hoffmann's body raced toward the road below, the rain muffled his scream. He was as good as dead already, but his arms and legs still pedaled as if he could magically take flight.

"Shit," I muttered.

He struck the ground, oddly angled, and I winced. A horn beeped, a car veered off course and came to a stop.

I turned away, lacking the stomach to see another body tonight. If I'd reacted faster, had gaged his state of mind better, he wouldn't be dead. My temper had put the fear of God into him, and through it, I'd messed up our chance to get closure for the victims' families, my pack included.

Eli bounced against the railing and slammed his hands against the metal frame. "Dammit, Ali."

"I tried, but he was so fast." I ran my hand through my hair. "I thought he'd changed his mind. You glamoured him, right? You had him under control."

"Until that klutz came charging out." He pointed his thumb

49

behind him at the waiter. "I lost concentration for a second. Fuck." He punched the railing again.

"That's it," the waiter shouted. "I'm calling the police."

Clutching his bottle under his arm, he stepped over the dark reddish puddle and hurried inside. As if the people in the cars below wouldn't have been heating up the phone lines to the cops already.

"Is Max dead?" Jack shuffled closer. "Like, for real?"

"We're on the tenth floor. What do you think?" I gave him a pissed look. "What are you doing here anyway? I told you to wait in the car."

"I got bored." He peered over the railing, whooped at the mayhem, and only then lifted his face again. "Is this the waiter's fault? Want me to rough him up?"

"Just be quiet for a moment." Eli shoved Jack aside with his flat hand. "Vulture."

"What the hell, man." The demon stumbled and fell onto his ass into a shallow puddle. "I'm as upset as you are."

I got into a crouch and steepled my fingers in front of my nose, blocking out the scent of gas, wet earth, and Jack's fib, which had left in its wake the whiff of rotting melon. Guilt and regret didn't seem part of the demon's arsenal. That ghoul got off on the chaos. The chaos I'd caused with my rash threats.

"Shit, shit, shit," I mumbled.

If I'd been quicker, just by a fraction of a second, Hoffmann would be alive. If I hadn't nearly strangled him, he wouldn't have chosen death over my wrath. The only evidence of our investigation—gone. My future—gone. Presenting Parker with the killer was supposed to give me a chance at keeping my status. Without Hoffmann, my alpha wouldn't even have reason to keep me around. I'd be exiled.

Exiled.

Without the safety of a pack, I'd be a rogue, a criminal with a target on my back.

"Shit," I said again, louder this time.

"Hey, he's dead." Jack got up and edged closer while staying outside Eli's reach. "Isn't that what you wanted?"

Maybe it was what *he'd* wanted. At first, Jack's enthusiasm for our hunt had seemed like an endearing quality, but I was all out of sympathy. Time was dripping away, and not only was I without the body of our killer, I still wasn't closer to being able to explain Heidi's death to my pack.

"We had questions for him, shitbrain." Eli bulleted forward and shoved him again. "Why did he kill Heidi? Was he responsible for more murders? Was he working alone?"

Jack stopped himself from falling again by waving his arms. "Hey, *I* didn't kill the guy."

Eli turned and stomped toward me. "Come on. Let's go home."

"Not yet." I considered the demon. "If you knew Max enough to know we'd find him here, you know where he lives. Right?"

"Whaaat?" Jack touched his chest. "Why would I know that?"

"Nice try." A grim grin spread across my face. "You think by asking questions you won't trigger my nose with your lies?"

"Do this fast, okay?" Eli slapped my shoulder. "The cops will be on their way."

He disappeared into the bar. No crowd had assembled inside to watch the drama unfold, even though they had to have noticed us. Were the guests too jaded or too afraid to get involved in other people's business?

Jack's hair had formed a poodle crown, or rather, a bird's nest, and the outlandish urgency that accompanied his movements had left his body.

I lowered my voice. "The address, Jack."

"Fine." Jack stood, a dripping mess. Wrapping his wool coat tighter around himself, he evaded my gaze. "I don't know the address, but I can show you."

"You're not coming with us." Christ, that guy kept pushing my patience. "Just give me the address. Now."

"I don't know the name of the road. Seriously. I'd know it if I saw it. It's in the flower quarter. You know, like the ad for the Flower King of Silverton?" He lifted both hands and swayed. "*For roses, red, or dahlias, pink, come and see the Flower Ki-i-i-ing.*"

He finished the tune with limp jazz hands and a sheepish smile.

Spending another ten minutes in his company would kill me, or more likely him, but the sandman's death was my fault. His home might hold clues as to his motive.

"Fine, come." I walked toward the bar. "If you get my car dirty, you'll pay for the cleaning."

I zoomed through the bar, not meeting the furtive glances cast by the patrons of this establishment, and then down the stairs—keeping at least ten paces ahead of the annoying demon. Not that outrunning Jack's company would ease my guilt, but it might enable me to keep my shit together so that I didn't accidentally kill him.

We ran into Eli at the bottom of the stairs.

"Found his wallet." He held it into the air. "Driver's license says he lives down Brock."

"That's nowhere near the flower quarter." I reached under Jack's collar and dragged him closer. "Care to explain?"

He retracted his head and neck like a tortoise. "That's his old address. Trust me. He lives in the flower quarter. I promise."

Again, I smelled no lie, but I checked Eli's face for reassurance. "What do you want to do?"

Sirens approached at top speed and with a fanfare of flashing lights.

"Come on." Eli waved us along. "Let's get out of here."

Silverton cops knew to approach crime scenes with a delay, or they'd be stuck with plenty of unexplainable evidence that would end up hurting their heads. Pentagrams, guys strong enough to be on PCP, smells they couldn't describe—the head-in-the-sand approach was easier.

At least, that was how Florian had explained it. He was a P.I., so he should know.

Weird that he and his brother should have picked such similar occupations.

A handful of cop cars shot past the three vehicles that had lined up by the intersection, either hindered in their journey by Hoffmann's body or distracted by their own morbid curiosity. If Eli didn't possess vampire speed or glamour, he would have never had the chance to search Hoffmann unnoticed.

Luck, caution, and the humans' desire to rationalize away the inexplicable helped us keep our existence secret.

Back in the Volvo, Eli wiped his phone dry before dialing and spoke in a hushed tone.

"Are you keeping my car clean?" I checked the rearview mirror to catch Jack's attention and took off as another cop car pulled up past my vehicle.

We went the other way.

"I'm using my coat as a seat cover." Jack beamed. "I keep my word."

His *wet* coat. Fan-fucking-tastic. After tonight, the seats would never be the same. The odor of the mold that would no doubt soon grow inside them already formed a lingering stench in my nose.

"Thanks, Clarence." Eli shoved his phone into his jacket pocket and pushed aside a wet streak of blond hair. "Hoffmann did live on Brock Road, but his apartment is now the home of Anna Levell, a human. Good chance he moved out and didn't update his details."

"Flower quarter then?" I asked.

Eli shot a nasty look over his shoulder, and I could practically hear Jack swallow.

"Trust me." Yet Jack no longer sounded as confident.

For his sake and ours, he'd better be right.

In stark contrast to the center of town with its fluorescent signs, the flower quarter was drowning in darkness, and light was even sparser on the road with what Jack insisted was Hoffmann's home.

We parked outside the midsize rancher that, like the rest of the buildings, looked asleep. I unfastened my seatbelt and took a deep breath.

"I know, I know." Jack waved me off. "'*Stay in the car, Jack.*' I will."

Eli scoffed quietly. His mood had taken a dent since Hoffmann's demise. After I nearly choked the guy to death, Eli could be excused for thinking I deliberately let Hoffmann fall. Maybe I did, subconsciously. While I wasn't sorry the guy was dead, I regretted hurting our chances of getting to the bottom of the sandman's motivation. Why did Hoffmann target Heidi? She'd never done anyone any harm. Her tough demeanor had been a façade. Anyone with half a brain would have seen that.

"Actually, I was going to ask if Hoffmann lived with anyone." I stared at the house, checking for movement. "A girlfriend or a mother?"

"No." Jack shrugged. "First, he was gay. And aside from a quick screw in a backroom, he didn't date."

"How do you know about this place? Were you friends?"

"I..."

I shifted in my seat to regard him closely.

"What can I say?" Jack's grin showed no sign of embarrassment. "He was a looker, and in case you're wondering, sex in backrooms is surprisingly comfortable."

"Exactly no one was wondering," I muttered.

Eli and I opened the doors in sync, just when Jack slapped our headrests.

"There." He pointed at the neighbor's bottom window. "See that black doodah above the frame? I think that's a camera."

I leaned across my steering wheel for a closer look, but Eli's superior night vision had me beat again.

"So it is." He glimpsed over his shoulder. "Is there a back door?"

Jack placed a finger against his jaw in a theatrical thinker's pose. "I don't think so."

"Right. Give me a sec." Eli's blur raced across the front yard and leaped at the device before his passenger door had clunked shut.

"Thanks," I said and followed Eli out.

"No pro—"

My door falling into the lock cut Jack off.

I arrived at the house just as Eli withdrew his pick from the lock. He let me enter first, then slowly closed the door.

"When we're done here, we're going to ditch Jack." He'd lowered his voice, even though the demon was out of earshot.

"Fine by me." I nodded. "He's a ghoul. And why didn't he tell us just how close he'd been to Hoffmann?"

"Because we wouldn't have let him join us." Eli skimmed the dark space with narrowed eyes. "My main worry is that he's in the business of selling information. I don't want our investigation to come to light before I know the facts."

"Neither do I." I turned on the light switch and took in the bare hallway, painted a faint yellow. "Assuming this is really Hoffmann's place, what are we looking for?"

"We'll know it once we find it."

Inside the living room, the furniture was modern, and the sofa had that real-leather sheen. Eli darted across the room, tossed the sleek throw-pillows onto the ground, stuck his hands under the seat cushions, and even kneeled to check under the black cabinet that lined the feature wall. The next second, he'd left the room to continue his search elsewhere.

I approached a watercolor of a windmill inside a metal frame that hung above the cabinet. Metal frames were unusual enough to warrant a second look, but it was one of Florian's stories that now made me draw up a chair and examine the frame's patterned surface.

From the back of the house, shuffling sounds and clangs indicated that Eli truly left no stone unturned.

Maybe I'd beat him to it. The purpose of guards, and of the patterns they exhibited, was to magically shape energy into the desired effect, including an extra dash of speed and protection against trespassers. Hopefully, this particular guard served as an invisibility shield hiding Hoffmann's motive.

"Find anything?" Eli returned from his search and stood beside the chair.

Sadly he saw no reason to put his hand on my leg or ass for support, but then my broad frame didn't look like I was in need of aid. Against his slender figure, I was an oaf. Story of my life. Wide shoulders and overdeveloped muscles were common among werewolves. No matter how often I tried to slim down, my bone structure couldn't be fixed with protein shakes or zero carbing.

"Did Florian tell you about that one case, where he and Ivy searched a demon's house and discovered a hidden drawer?" I leaned precariously across the case with one hand against the wall. "A metal guard had concealed it, but Ivy stopped the guard's magic with one touch."

"Guards can do that?" Eli scratched his head. "I own a guard that keeps the sun from frying me during the day, and I've seen one that can stop glamour, but I've never heard of anyone making hidey holes with them."

I traced the faint lines inside the frame to their inlet points. So far, Eli had driven the investigation, and it was time I pulled my weight. Of course, I'd look a right idiot if I was wrong.

"Here's something." I pressed my thumb into the metal at the top left starting point of the crisscrossing lines. "Anything?"

"Hmm? Oh, maybe." He stuck his head between the cabinet and my precariously tilted body. "It's not a hidden drawer, but I don't remember this box being here when we first entered the room."

I pushed away from the wall and spotted a document holder the size of a bread box.

"Let me open—" He furrowed his brows. "Are you coming down, or is the air better up there?"

Using his shoulder as support, I jumped off the chair. My landing was steady, and my weight didn't shake the building's foundations. For once, I'd done good and contributed to our investigation.

"How do you know about this magic stuff anyway?" Eli fumbled with the case's lock.

"Ivy gave us lectures about guards. How to recognize what they do, how to protect against them, that sort of thing. She knows her stuff."

"Yeah." He heaved the box to a coffee table and took a seat on the sofa. "You attended every one of her lessons and took notes, didn't you?"

"Make fun of me all you want, but my study skills paid off, didn't they?" I sauntered across the hardwood floor and took a seat next to him.

"So they did. Still, just because she's Florian's business partner doesn't mean you have to do as she says."

"I didn't attend her lessons for Florian." The words shot from my mouth like a poison-soaked arrow.

"Whoa, hey. I didn't mean anything by that." Eli hung his head. "And by the way, I'm sorry things between you didn't work out."

"He's happy, and that's half the battle, right?" I'd forced my tone into a one-eighty, and I almost believed myself.

"What about the other half?"

I flared my nose as my only response. Being around Florian had taught me a certain serenity in the handling of vampires. Still, where Florian's goofiness was a minor annoyance, Eli's inquisitiveness had the potential to max out my patience. He was...challenging.

"Let's see." Eli pulled a couple of thin folders out of the box without letting me see them. "Why did you do it then? Learn about guards?"

He was a persistent fella, I couldn't deny that.

"Because Ivy isn't just a great teacher; she's the boss's girl, and she rules the roost in my house."

"You don't like her?"

"Of course I do."

"Can I assume then that you don't have a problem with non-wolves, you know, those of us who run on two feet rather than four?"

"You don't run on all fours?" I shook my head in mock pity. "Hell, I don't even want to know you."

"Funny." He nudged me with his shoulder.

"I try."

"Right, let's have a look." He leafed through the papers and handed me the sheets as he read them. "Hoffmann was organized."

That much had been clear from the furniture. Everything was neat, without clutter or frill. Nevertheless, Hoffmann had put a good deal of money into his sparse décor. Everything, from the simple rug on the hardwood floor to the wall clock, was well made. The TV and his stereo carried the names of big brands, and even the two magazines in the rack next to the table were glossy and aspirational.

"He also had money." I turned my attention to the invoices and order forms in my hand, but my focus didn't persist.

Eli sat close to me, our legs touching. A strand of hair had fallen into his face, and I was itching to tuck it behind his ear.

"I'm trying to make sense of these." He lifted the sheets in a helpless gesture. "All I can tell from the paperwork is Hoffmann was involved in a company called *Hard and Sweet*."

"Like *Hard and Sweet* sex toys?"

"I like 'em, sure." He blew me a kiss. "But I really think we should keep our head in the game."

A jolt shot through my dick, and I whacked him over the head with my stack of documents. Men as handsome as Eli shouldn't tease men like me.

He rubbed his head, even though my thin stack of paper hadn't exactly smacked a hole into his skull.

"Funny." I mimicked his voice and didn't even hide my grin. "What's *Hard and Sweet?*"

"God." He fanned himself with the folder in his hand. "You're killing me."

"I mean the company, Eli. How is it connected to Heidi's death?"

"I don't know that it is. It's a candy bar company. I'm seeing they have a delivery scheduled from their Silverton factory to the old mill by Lawton's Bridge in the morning—at least that's what this e-mail says." He punched the air as if it were a solid wall. "Fuck. Fuck, fuck, fuck, fuck."

"What is it?" I tried to catch a glimpse of the page he was holding up, but I saw nothing on it that would account for his outburst.

"Okay." Eli's gaze intensified. "But fair warning. What I'm about to tell you could get you killed."

His tone made clear his words weren't an exaggeration.

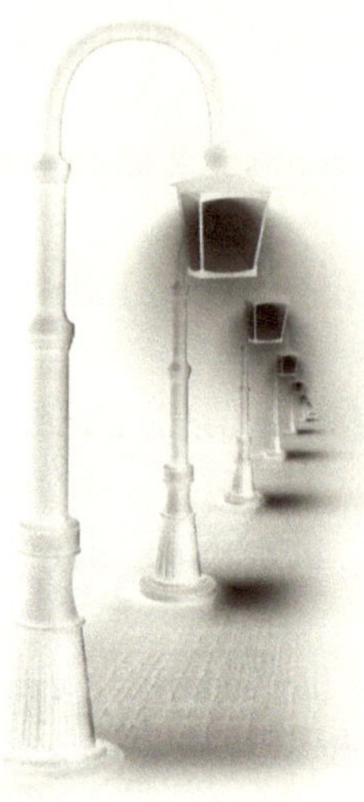

CHAPTER SEVEN

Whatever information Eli had uncovered, it had to be huge. He used understatement to get his point across. A threat to my life would be more than idle banter.

"That serious?" I shifted around on the sofa. "What did you find? More importantly, who'd want to kill me?"

"Me, if you tell anyone." Eli's expression was a serious as I'd ever seen. "Lawton's Bridge, the same Lawton's Bridge the shipment of candy bars is headed to, is the super-secret location of the IEA's portal to Alethia."

"You're kidding." I rubbed the area above my nose, as if the sensation would cause my questions to fall into a neat order of priority. "You have your own portal?"

"Sure. We work for the kinlords of Alethia. They can't cross over to our world, but they still need their earthly pleasures. Don't worry, the portal is guarded."

"I didn't know candy bars were such a huge thing with kinlords."

"Yeah, me neither. They're typically more interested in receiving human slaves than sugary snacks." He swayed forward and backward, pensively. "Putting aside the fact of how Hoffmann found out about the portal, how could he hope to get past our guards? Why not use one of the legitimate trading portals? That's their purpose—to bring those nice Alethians their gossip magazines and breakfast cereals, and provide kin over here with amulets and other magical paraphernalia."

"True." I nudged him. "You have connections, right? Can't you find someone who knows why a kinlord would green-light a shipment of candy bars through the super-secret IEA portal?"

"Maybe. But it's not really a call I want to make."

"And I hate to push, but I'm running out of time." I interlinked my fingers as I stared at the wall clock. "I have three hours left, dude. Do you know what will happen to me if I return empty-handed after all this? I'll be kicked out."

"Surely not."

"Yeah, I will. Parker will have no choice."

"Fine. Okay, but... Oh crap." He rummaged in his back pocket and pulled out a flat polished rock. "Scooch out of sight."

"Out of sight of what?"

"Just scooch."

While I moved to the outer edge of the sofa, Eli whispered something. The stone didn't magically transform into a carriage, nor did it take flight. Whatever he'd hoped would happen, wasn't.

He spoke again, louder now.

"Do you two need to be alone?" I grinned.

"Shh." He waved off. "Give him a second."

A hiss so quiet a human might have missed it came from his hand. Above the stone, floating as a holographic projection, an exceedingly handsome face appeared, with a distinguished trimmed mustache and kind eyes.

Already several steps up from Eli's one other source I'd met: Jack.

"Eli." The man raised his eyebrows. "How nice to hear from you."

He was older than me, but then, it was tough to be sure when it came to kin. His skin was dark—not Mediterranean or African, but rather Asian like me—and unnaturally smooth.

"Thank you, sir." Eli scrunched his face. "Please accept my apologies for not getting in touch sooner. My work has kept me busy. I'm trying to make you proud."

No, Eli wasn't. Not in the least.

Even if the dude on the other side of the connection had been a werewolf, he wouldn't be able to pick up Eli's fib from a distance. I, on the other hand, got the scent delivered in full 3D—and dammit, even Eli's lies smelled mighty fine.

"You could kill your director and take his post," the stranger said. "That would make me proud indeed." He laughed not in an evil but rather a jolly way.

"I don't believe Lathan would let me survive that." Eli gave a tight smile.

"No, he wouldn't. Now. How can I be of service, sweet boy?"

The man's accent was faint and impossible to pinpoint, but it didn't take much to deduce that this was Mehmet. And Eli had him on magical speed dial.

"A serial killer has been killing kin across Silverton, and I'm looking through the killer's papers," Eli said. "He has a cargo of candy bars due to be shipped to Alethia through the IEA's portal. I can't figure out how a sandman would know of the portal, who would allow him access, or why he wouldn't use the legitimate sales portals."

"This is why you contacted me?" The vampire kinlord's shoulders sagged. "You disappoint me."

"Unfortunately, the issue is both important and time-critical, sir."

"Have vampires died at this killer's hands?"

"Not yet, as far as I know. To be honest, I'm not even sure the shipment and the murders are connected."

"Then why do you care?" Mehmet shook his head. "Why should *I* care?"

"Director Vanguard believes there is no serial killer and I intend to prove him wrong." Eli's voice held steady with patience and a lot of respect. "Sir, this is a career-making case."

"Ah." Mehmet tapped his nose with his finger. "I understand. To answer one of your questions, using the official portals is prohibitively expensive. Believe me, I know. These portals are also heavily guarded."

"Okay, so they don't want to pay, but they also don't want to get into it with twenty or thirty guards. That would leave the IEA's secret portal. It's less well protected."

"It seems you have your answer."

"Still, risking the wrath of the IEA is a lot of effort to ship candy bars to Alethia."

Mehmet frowned. "Candy bars? But what for?"

"That's what we're trying to figure out."

"We?" Mehmet glanced around.

I tilted further out of view until my ribs pressed against the sofa's armrest.

"We at the IEA," Eli said quickly.

"You're not asking the right question, Eli." Mehmet bared his teeth, showing some pretty fearsome canines. "Overcoming the Agency's guards is a minor problem. I wonder who is going to accept shipment at our end."

"Is that something you may be able to discover, sir?" Eli brushed his hair behind his ear. "I'm sure you command the best spies in Alethia."

"That I do." The kinlord pointed his chin up. "Very well. I will have an answer for you soon."

"I owe you, sir. Thank you."

The face disappeared, and Eli stared at the blank wall.

"Are you all right?" I sat up.

He glanced at his hand. "Yes, thanks. I just hate having to constantly be subservient to him."

"That sucks. But having his support is important in your line of work, isn't it?"

"Yeah. He's the second most powerful kinlord." Eli got out his cell and typed for a few minutes. "Our guards are well trained, but I doubled the manpower for the next few days, just in case."

"Is all this necessary?" I peered at the heavy drapes that covered only one half of a large living-room window. "The candy bars are his business. Maybe illegal, sure, but I don't see the connection to the deaths we're investigating. Besides, Hoffmann's dead."

"Doesn't mean the company he owns is. And yes, maybe the two are unconnected, but I can't rule anything out. Maybe the business is a front for smugglers and the kids saw something they shouldn't have seen. They were killed in different ways so as not to draw attention?"

"Sounds far-fetched."

"Maybe. Still, Mehmet threw up an interesting question. How does a sandman develop contacts in Alethia, you know, kin powerful enough to have access to the kinlords' gates?"

"True. It's tough to meet across the realms. There's no crossover, no chance meeting with an Alethian on a train or in a pub." I snapped my fingers. "Maybe there's an app for it."

"Hell, don't even joke about that." He chortled.

"Why did Mehmet have his fangs out? You don't, and your... sister doesn't either."

He awarded my effort to not mention his brother with a smile. "Here, we try to blend in with humans. In Alethia, it pays to look scary."

"Mehmet looked quite friendly until he showed his fangs."

"Friendly's not a word I'd use to describe him." Eli skimmed his gaze across the walls and even turned to the door behind him.

"What are you looking for?" I asked.

"I don't know." Eli opened and closed his hand repeatedly. "If Hoffmann's a psychopathic serial killer, shouldn't we find souvenirs in this house? He hides invoices in a guarded box, but no mementos of his kills?"

"I don't think there's a rule by which all serial killers must keep the ears of their victims."

"Maybe not." He chewed his lip and stared off into the distance again. "Maybe I'm just looking for reasons to connect his business to the killings, because it's our only lead."

"We know he did it. We have his face on camera." I rubbed my leg, which suffered from stiffness both due to the nature of our mission and due to the weather I'd had to endure. "Before you stopped me from choking Hoffmann, he told me he was sorry *they* had to die."

The insecure flickers in Eli's expression faded.

"They," I repeated. "Plural. He was the killer, and Heidi wasn't his first victim. Maybe he owns another place where he keeps his killing stuff. The guns and the poisons and the other murder weapons he used."

"It's possible." Eli retrieved his phone and dialed. "Clarence. ... No, the guy we were looking for is dead. ... Accident, yes. ... I really don't care what he thinks." Eli mouthed 'Vanguard' and rolled his eyes. "Anyway, can you look into a candy bar company called *Hard and Sweet* for me? Partners, finances, assets, that kind of thing. ... Awesome. Also check for buildings in the name of Max Hoffmann. ... Thanks, dude."

He hung up.

"The director making trouble again?" I asked.

"No more than usual."

"Is Vanguard a demon?"

"That's a big, fat yes." Eli tilted his head. "Thinks being one of Lathan's chosen makes him special. Not sure what kind of demon he is, but his bark's worse than his bite."

"That was my assessment." I scoffed. "If he had as much power as he pretends, you'd be cleaning the floor."

The entry door rattled, and footsteps approached from the hallway. Eli and I exchanged a glance. A second later, he was stuffing papers into his pockets while I shoved the document holder behind the sofa, out of sight.

"Are you done, Eli?" Jack appeared, hiding his hands inside his pockets. "I thought we could go to a club or something, get a drink or talk shop. Whatever you want."

That guy needed a reality check. I understood fan-boying over Eli, but the demon's obsession was getting close to stalker behavior.

With his jaw tensed, Eli stared at the demon. "Didn't we tell you to stay in the car?"

"I was bored." Jack skimmed the table and floor, and then stepped forward. "Found anything?"

"Sadly, nothing at all." Eli shook his head, as if deeply disappointed by his failure.

I got up and circled around Jack, forcing his gaze to follow me. "Maybe you can help us. Did you set up any deals between your friend Max and any underground bigwigs recently?"

"No." Jack wasn't lying. "Not for years, but I didn't have to either. Max had his regular clientele and wasn't exactly ambitious, you know. He wasn't one to climb the ladder."

"Okay. Personal question." I armed myself with my most innocent-looking smile. "Why did you want to accompany us in the first place?"

"What do you mean?"

"I'm saying it's late. Wouldn't you have preferred staying in bed, where it's warm and dry?"

Jack's bottom lip pushed forward. "You were the ones who asked about Max. I was just trying to be helpful."

"Bullshit." I shot forward, relying on my height and width to get to the truth. My smile was long gone.

"Okay, okay." Jack bowed his head. "I hoped you might hurt Max."

"You hoped?" I scoffed. "Did he break up with you or something?"

"Yes." His quiet word was barely audible.

Truth.

"Okay then." I stepped back, almost feeling sorry for the guy.

"Now let me ask *you* something. Why are we still here if you didn't find anything?" Jack asked. "Let's go, guys. I honestly thought IEA missions were more exciting than this."

"More exciting than death and chaos?" My voice sharpened again.

Eli's hand on my back immediately quenched the heat in my guts.

"Come on, you two," he said. "Time to go home."

We exchanged a covert glance. Whatever our next move, Jack wouldn't be a part of it. Too much effort, too little reward. Surely Eli had better contacts than him.

The rain had lessened, the lightning ceased. Yet Heidi was still dead, and I was still screwed. Maybe Clarence had found a new lead. We needed a break soon or my time with the pack would come to an end. A self-starter like Eli couldn't possibly understand why wolves like me feared being exiled. Aside from the inherent danger that came with going it alone, we were social animals by nature. Even though I hid in my office by day, I drew strength from the noise and bustle, and from our camaraderie. Shared runs through the woods bound us together, as did our common cause to keep our pack safe and strong. To give all this up was unthinkable.

While I drove in silence, Eli maintained a muted conversation with Jack. The vampire was a master of evading Jack's creepy come-ons. He probably had a lot of practice.

Fifteen minutes later, I parked outside Jack's house. "Thanks for your help."

At four in the morning, the streets here in the 'burbs remained devoid of people. Normal kin and humans alike would have gone to sleep hours ago, cycled through their REM stages without realizing there was one less sandman and one less werewolf in the world.

"You're welcome." Jack made no moves to get out, other than a teeth chatter to remind us he was wet and cold. "I know it didn't turn out the way you wanted, but at least Hoffmann's dead, right?"

"Right," I parroted. What a strange creature he was. "Anyway, good night."

He eyed the drizzle, which continued without entirely ceasing. "Yeah. Um. Hey, do you want to hang out? We could play cards."

"It's been a long day." Eli turned in his seat and for once, he shut his eyes to gather strength. "Go home."

"Fine." The demon put on his coat, pushed the door open and climbed out, his bag clutched under his arm. "Nice to meet you, Ali."

"Uh-huh."

"Bye, Eli. Maybe we can do this again some time?"

Eli's hand formed a fist, but he retained his outward calm. "Sure."

The demon seemed appeased and slapped my rooftop twice before closing the door.

"Get us away from here before he changes his mind." Eli shook his head. "What the hell's wrong with him?"

"He's in love with you." I grinned. "You should feel flattered."

Someone ripped open Eli's door.

Hell, what did it take to get rid of that guy?

"What now?" I asked, annoyed.

Then the door next to me disappeared, too. A large, hairy fist soared toward me and crunched into my nose.

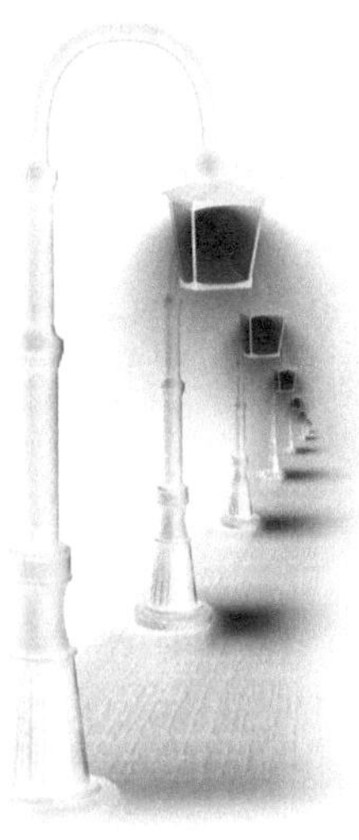

CHAPTER EIGHT

Pain flared inside my nostrils. The seat belt kept me strapped in, giving my opponent's fist perfect access to land on my ear. My head buzzed, my eyes lost focus, and I clambered to free myself. The moment the belt fastener clicked open, I got dragged out of the car. I kicked out—and struck a knee.

A man hunched and held his leg. He was shorter and wider than me. Dark veins marbled his button eyes, and his breath stank of whiskey. If he was hoping for quick cash or to jack my car, he'd soon regret it.

"You didn't think this through, did you?" I asked as I weaved out of his way.

The guy's jaw muscles pulsed. He opened his mouth a fraction, then flicked his gaze to the side the same moment his arm exploded toward me.

I deflected his attack and landed a blow of my own on his chin. The splat upon contact didn't last nearly long enough to lure a smile from me. His force and hardiness suggested he was a demon. Certainly not a human.

Maybe they weren't just a couple of petty thieves.

"What do you want?" I shoved the guy against the side of my car.

He pushed back, but not so hard as to threaten my balance.

"You've been putting your nose in other people's business." My opponent danced in front of me boxer-style, feigning left and right, holding his hands in loose fists to cover his face. "My boss doesn't like that."

An organized attack. Surely Eli and I had done something right to evoke such a violent response.

"Who's your boss?" I grabbed him by the belt and collar and slammed him against the side of my car. Water splashed into my mouth—dirty, filthy-tasting water—and I spat on the ground.

My attacker hung limp against my Volvo.

"I said, who's your boss?" While I tightened a hand around my opponent's throat, I checked across the roof to see how my two companions fared.

Jack wasn't anywhere to be seen, while Eli missiled blows and kicks at his two assailants so fast, only the yells and curses of the men gave away how much hurt he was dispensing.

"Let go and I'll tell you." My guy yanked on my hand with a slow awkwardness.

I moved in to pin him tight without giving him a way out. His eyes held too much spunk yet for believable answers.

Fine by me. Although my wolf didn't feel challenged by the demon, I'd been dying to hit something for a while now.

I exploited his immobility to land a perfect jab on his chin, then followed it up with a thorough blow to his guts. He wheezed and nudged me—into the arms of a pretty brunette.

"Sorry." My apology was a reflex. I even found time to smile before she smacked her knuckles into my eye.

The dull thudding at the point of impact took second fiddle to a punch to my kidney from the guy.

One demon I didn't mind, but being ganged up on offended my

sense of fairness. I grabbed the man by his shirt collar and the woman's thin arm, and catapulted the two into each other.

Button-Eyes' head rammed into her breasts, by all accounts a soft landing. She peeled him off her body and came at me for another punch. Her tight pants didn't restrict her range of motion in the least.

"Don't make me hurt you." I sidestepped her first two attempts. "I just need your boyfriend to answer a few questions, and you two can go."

"Chauvinist. Pig." The brunette pulled her bright red lips into a nasty curve. "He's not my boyfriend."

The tip of her worker's boot connected with my shin.

"Shit," I pushed through my grinding teeth.

At the same moment, her nails clawed into my neck.

Traces of fire burned along my skin.

My female friends were no wallflowers, and I'd witnessed Ivy dish out a fair amount of ass-kicking, but I'd never struck a woman.

"Hit her, for fuck's sake," Eli shouted.

"She's a woman." I fended her off enough to put space between us.

"For crying out loud. Man up and punch her already." Eli sounded oddly amused.

He stood by my car's bonnet. No sight of his attackers.

The woman grinned. "Sucks being a chauvinistic furball, doesn't it?"

How had she known I was a werewolf? I rarely went out, so it was unlikely she'd have spotted me with better known members of my pack. Someone must have told her.

Interesting.

She kicked at my knee with her heel and rammed her fingers toward my eyes.

I turned my face away at the last minute, but my leg caught the full brunt. "Who are you clowns?"

And where the hell was the manual that covered male-on-female combat?

She gripped my collar and pushed me—into her partner's incoming fist.

I dove to the side so his hand merely grazed my cheek. The glancing blow still hurt.

"I've told you what you need to know." He swung again. "Consider this beating your warning."

"We'll see about that," I mumbled and gripped his shoulder.

Momentum carried him toward the woman, and his fist crunched into her tanned face instead of mine.

"Idiot!" She held her nose.

"Come on, Ali," Eli heckled. "Thought we're on a clock."

"Dammit," I mumbled, but he was right. This fight had turned into a polite skirmish, an embarrassment even. Besides, my friendly approach wasn't getting me the answers I was looking for.

My next karate chop to the back of my opponent's neck felled him, and I planted my boot squarely on his jaw. In the same instant, I took out the woman with a well-placed jab.

She dropped to the ground beside her partner.

Look at me. Sneaked out without Parker's permission, worked with the IEA, and now I'd hit a woman. Tonight, my principles were taking a few serious body blows.

Eli had draped his front over the bonnet. "Nicely done. I'm impressed with your stamina."

His mid-length hair hung in straight strands, raindrops pearled on his cheeks, and his jacket had lost what little shape a tailor had once given it, yet the cocky smile on his face blessed him with a summery glow. Damn, he had that cute look down pat.

Maybe emboldened by the rush of adrenaline, I grinned. "You're not the first guy to tell me that."

He laughed and straightened. "You tease."

Yeah, right.

"You took your time with the chick, though." Eli rounded the car and crouched low to check my attackers. "Are all werewolves sexist?"

"We're not." Except we kind of were. "We're protective."

"Uh-huh." He didn't sound convinced.

"Besides, our pack has had to accept that women are every bit as tough, cunning, and mean as the rest of us. We're slowly moving into the twenty-first century."

"Wonderful. Then why the hesitation?"

"I'm not good with change." I found a semi-dry tissue in my pants pockets and used it to rub the dirt from my coat. "It's a weakness, I admit."

The stain, visible even on my drenched gray fabric, only spread. At least the rain had finally stopped. Maybe I'd make it through the night without developing gills.

Eli patted the guy's pockets. The demon groaned—and Eli snapped his neck.

The crack iced my next words, which got caught in my throat. I stared at the soggy mess in my hand, at the mud spot on my chest, and tightened my fist around the tissue.

"It's tough to move on if you're stuck in the same place." Eli got to his feet, seemingly unaffected by his kill. "I thought tonight would help you get out of your comfort zone."

He dragged the body around the car, where presumably two more corpses formed the early stage of a heap.

"Is that why you asked for my help?" I wiped the water off my face and stuffed the tissue back in my pocket to be disposed of later. "Am I a charity case?"

He returned to stand not two feet away, close enough for me to see the small puffs of air from his mouth before the breeze stole them away.

"No." His arm twitched, and for a second, I thought he might touch me, but I must have misread him. He leaned his head to the side. "I thought it might be fun."

"And?" I raised my eyebrows.

"Turns out I was right." He marched past me, leaving me with the whiff of his wet clothes and the faint, yet much more scintillating scent of ocean freshness from his skin.

"Hang on." I grabbed the tail end of his jacket. "You're not going to kill her, are you?"

"You're still looking out for the woman. That's cute." His glance bounced off her soaked, crumpled form. "What's your plan? The IEA doesn't run a prison. You want to call the cops?"

Hardly. The human police wouldn't know what to do with kin of the demon persuasion.

"At least let her tell us who sent her." I turned on my heels. "By the way, where's Jack?"

Eli leaned in. "No clue. Maybe they killed him?"

"You could sound a little less hopeful. He probably ran home to hide." I cocked my chin at the woman. "Let's see what she says."

The female demon moved slowly and raised her head, which was draped by clingy streaks of hair. She was fairly pretty, or would have been if her makeup had been more waterproof. Eli pinched the front of her sodden sweater in his hand and pulled her up against the car as if she weighed nothing. She swayed, but he held steady.

My back and limbs felt ice-cold. I could get used to sun, snow, and windy conditions, but rain was the worst. Even though it had stopped, it had soaked through every fiber of my clothes and almost into my flesh.

"Who hired you?" Eli asked.

"Hired me?" The brunette's dazed gaze darted into the darkness. "No one."

"Lie." I added a growl. "This is taking too long. Can't you glamour her?"

Eli tilted his head and then lowered his lids a fraction. "I can try."

The woman's features slackened in an instant. Her mild smile and moist eyes gave her a crazed expression.

"Who do you work for?" I asked in a low voice.

"Lathan." She spoke the name softly, yet it sucker-punched me straight in the gut.

I shouldn't be surprised the demon kinlord was behind the violence, but the mention of his name gave me the chills anyway.

"Why's he targeting us?" I prodded her shoulder. "What's his plan?"

"He's coming."

A cough sounded from further up the sidewalk.

Her beguiled smile faltered. "Hang on, what?"

"I've got it." I nodded at Eli and went to check out the sound.

Jack lay sprawled on his back, eyes glazed, yet still holding on to the strap of his backpack.

I gripped his arm and pulled him to his feet. "You all right?"

He swung his free hand as if to hit me.

I side-stepped the blow. "What the hell are you doing?"

"Oh, it's you." He wiped blood off his fat lip. There was nothing jolly about him now. "Sorry. I got knocked down. Are *you* all right?"

"Yes, I'm fine." I dragged him toward my car and pointed at the pile of dead men lying one on top of the other, in an array of unnatural positions. "Know any of them?"

"Yeah, they're demons. Are they dead?"

That guy was so stupid it was a miracle his brain had worked out how to breathe.

"Fuck." Eli jumped back, letting go of the female demon.

I deposited Jack against the Volvo and headed to the other side of the car. The woman had fallen to the ground, where she lay gurgling, with something dark oozing from her body.

Eli pointed. "Blood."

"No shit, Sherlock." I threw my hands up in the air. "What did you do?"

The woman wheezed a few times before her eyes rolled and

she stopped moving. A knife handle projected from her stomach, its blade embedded deep.

I slowly tilted my head at Eli. "You were supposed to make her tell us who sent her."

We'd messed up again. We'd started out with four suspects—four mouths to tell us who hired them—and now they were all dead.

Eli was breathing hard, his eyes dark as the night. Dammit. He was struggling not to let his blood frenzy get the upper hand.

I dragged the brunette's body behind the car, where it joined the men's unmoving shapes. Had this been an ambush meant for Eli and me specifically, or had Lathan discovered Jack was helping us and wanted all of us beaten to a pulp? The female demon had been pretty specific about her boss's name. That, in turn, would imply the demon kinlord himself had been doing business with Max Hoffmann.

But to what end? To munch on candy bars? And how did this connect to Heidi's death?

I took the coat off one of the male attackers and draped it over the woman's wound. Maybe the IEA had a clean-up crew. If not, we'd created one hell of a headline in the paper. Either way, four dead demons who'd tried to take us out wouldn't weigh on my conscience all that much.

"Better?" I joined Eli and almost placed my hand on the back of his neck.

Almost. Would he welcome my touch? Physical contact seemed second nature to him, so maybe he would. But what if he thought I was coming on to him? He'd already had to deal with Jack's unwanted advances. The last thing I wanted was to make the night worse for him.

"Yeah." He took a few shallow breaths. "I thought I had better control over myself."

I lifted my arm. Gently arranged my hand on his shoulder, close to his collar.

He didn't flinch.

Maybe he hadn't even noticed. Even though the rain had stopped its relentless attack, the red-stained puddle by his feet remained. It was possible that staying sane so close to the remnants of blood took up his full concentration.

"You *are* controlling it." I brushed my thumb over his cheek to remove a speck of blood. "Any other vampire would have lost it by now."

"She killed herself." Eli shook his head, and his hair flung a water droplet onto my hand. "That bitch went and stabbed herself rather than tell me what she knew."

"If you're all done making out, I think I'll go home now." Jack wrapped his jacket tightly around himself and held his backpack clasped in his hand. "This hasn't been the fun night you'd promised me at all."

I quickly dropped my arm and shrugged. "Write to your congressman."

Jack wheeled around and stalked off toward his house.

"Should we just let him go?" Despite his words, Eli made no attempt to stop the demon. "If Lathan sent these attackers, he might send others. The kinlord clearly knows Jack's been helping us."

"I still can't believe the woman killed herself." I peered at my car, which was hiding her body from sight. "You told me the kinlords wield real power here, but... Man."

"It's not the first time I've witnessed someone choosing suicide over a kinlord's wrath. Except that time, it had been a vampire who'd fallen foul of Mehmet."

"Come on." I nudged Eli toward the car. "Let's get out of here."

"Jack was almost right," Eli said once we were seated. "This hasn't at all turned out the way I'd hoped. It must be close to five, and we don't have anything to show for it."

He didn't have to remind me.

"I thought we were out of leads. I was about to suggest we head home." I started the car and caught my cut lip in the rearview mirror—although it was the mixed-in filth that really irked me. "But this attack must mean something."

"We have the documents we found at Hoffmann's place. Maybe Mehmet can shed more light soon."

"Yeah, maybe."

"Silver lining then." Looking entirely uninjured, Eli pressed the touch-screen on his phone with some force.

"What is it?"

"I don't want you to think I'm palling around with my grand-sire." Eli squinted at his display. "I don't even know the man. I'm only pretending like I'm his to command."

I surreptitiously wiped the dirt off my face with my sleeve but didn't get it as clean as I'd have liked. "I know."

"Without him, I wouldn't have my job. Besides, defying him would not be good for my health."

"That's beginning to dawn on me, yeah."

He stared ahead, evading my gaze.

"It's cool, man. Honest. I have to obey my alpha, too." I peeled off the curb and turned on the radio. "Even when I don't agree. You do what you gotta do. That's how things work."

"Clean up's on its way." Eli kept scrolling on his phone. "Hey, listen to this. Hoffmann's suicide has already hit the news."

"What are they saying?"

"The cops are tight-lipped, but the waiter's got a lot to say. He was going to save the poor fella, but a guest of the establishment got in the way."

I chuckled. "Jack's famous. What about us?"

"They didn't mention us." Eli was about to put his phone back into his pocket when it vibrated.

"I know Heidi's murderer is dead." My voice held, despite the continuing ache inside. "But why am I not getting a sense of closure?"

"Maybe you're not supposed to get closure when a person close to you dies." He tapped his display.

"Maybe."

He knew just as much about loss as I did.

I lowered the radio's volume. "Why did Hoffmann place Heidi outside our house? He must have suspected we had a camera. After all, he had one pointed at his own house."

"Maybe Hoffmann wasn't that bright. Oh." Eli waved his phone at me. "Clarence and the medical examiner have news. We officially have a cause of death for Heidi."

I tightened my hands around the steering wheel and set my jaw. "Hit me. Was it poison?"

"It's odd." He scratched his head. "Heidi, it turns out, was killed by a zucchini."

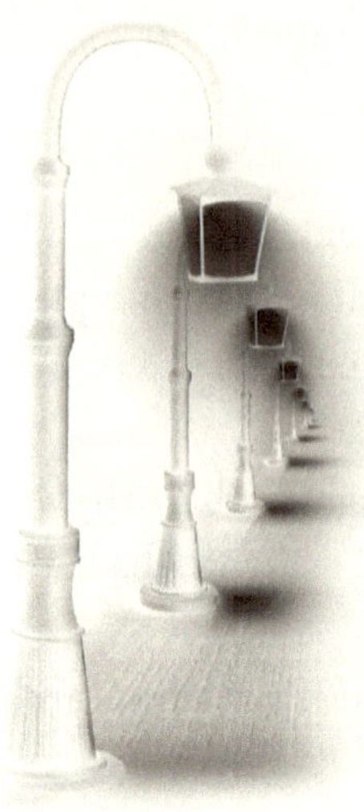

CHAPTER NINE

"What do you mean, Heidi was killed by a zucchini?" I glimpsed at Eli's dimple, highlighted by his mischievous grin.

"You'll find out." He shifted deeper into the passenger seat of my car.

I didn't mind him getting comfortable by my side. Didn't mind at all.

The silence that followed his mysterious news was relaxed enough. The impact of Heidi's death on me hadn't lessened, but it had been a long day, and I was tired of the pain inside. Relentlessly it puckered away in my ribcage, like a heart beating to its own rhythm. Maybe the ache would subside once I'd got justice for my girl. Once I'd uncovered all the answers. It was all I could do for her, but to make it that far, I needed my sanity. An outlet of some kind.

Eli's gallows humor was as effective a coping mechanism as any other.

Zucchinis aside, Lathan's name being mentioned had raised the stakes of our investigation. Often I'd wondered if his power wasn't so much magical as mythical. Being trapped in Alethia, having to rely on the generations of demons that had remained in Oldworld, should have castrated his influence. Yet the brunette who'd attacked me hadn't lied when she stated the kinlord's name.

"What are you making of this whole affair?" Eli crossed his arms. "And what about the woman saying, '*He's coming*'?"

"I have no idea." I let the buildings zip past me, too drained to focus on my surroundings. "What we do know is that Lathan's involved, and that gives me all sorts of unhappy feelings."

"Yeah." Eli took a large breath. "I gotta say, the past six months have felt like the calm before the storm. Things have been too quiet at the IEA, and Florian didn't mention any emergencies at your end either."

And here I was thinking no drama was a good thing.

"If Lathan's involved, any of our theories so far are too small. For him to send demons to warn us off means we're on to something. No one knows we found Hoffmann's papers about his company. So this must be about the murders."

"Lathan killing one of our wolves kind of makes sense." I drummed my finger against the steering wheel. "He was obsessed with Ivy for a long time. She's with Parker now, so a strike against our pack, just out of spite—that I get. But why would he kill other kin? And why kids?"

"I don't know, but I should have noticed there were no demon kids among the victims."

"Here's what I don't get. If our investigation's irking Lathan, why didn't he order our deaths? You're his archenemy's grandson, and I'm a werewolf. He can't have sentimental attachments."

"Good question. Maybe he's trying to avoid attracting any more attention."

"I hope that means that the rest of our werewolves are safe."

"I should think so. Only one kid per kin has died so far." Eli wiped his hands across his face. "Listen to me: *only* one." He scoffed. "How come we have more questions now than before we found Hoffmann?"

"Let's see if your friends have answers." I passed the barrier to the IEA's back entrance and parked in my spot just outside the door.

Eli was all business again the second we entered the IT department. "What's the what, Clarence?"

I shook out my clothes and sat on a chair to pick encrusted mud off my pant legs. The bits dropped into the wastebasket I'd commandeered, but the clean feeling I'd hoped for didn't set in. It had been a long time since I'd witnessed such a blustery night. The summer had been long and hot, and rain was badly needed—just not all in one night.

"So much to tell you, Chief." Clarence rubbed his red face. "First of all, Mina's blood analysis of the body's back."

The body. That was what Heidi was known as to those who hadn't met her.

"She died of..." He moved his face close to his computer screen. "A cucurbitacin derivative in highly concentrated form. Cucurbitacin is a natural toxin found in squashes and gourds."

Eli clicked his tongue in an I-told-you way. "As I said, she was killed by a zucchini."

"Kind of." Clarence tapped on his keyboard. "Cucurbitacin has been bred out of most fruit used for food, like zucchinis, but still occurs in wild varieties and is highly toxic. It's typically ingested, but very bitter."

"Why poison her? And with such a bizarre compound?" Eli traced his thumb over his chin. "All the other murders involved mundane killing methods. Many appeared to be accidents. But poisoning by zucchini is bizarre."

I tightened my dirty hands around my knees. Their discussion made sense on an objective level, but not on mine. Why would Heidi eat a zucchini? She wasn't exactly known for her love of vegetables.

I took a deep breath.

Hadn't been known. Dammit. I kicked the wastebasket.

It shook and toppled over.

"Sorry," I mumbled and bent over to slide its contents back where they belonged.

Clarence and Eli stopped talking, yet both made a point of not meeting my gaze.

Cowards. One smile, one smart-aleck comment, and my fist would finally find a home again. It wasn't just the wolf in me that longed for another good fight, except time was short already.

I moved the basket aside and stretched, crossing my hands behind my head. Every muscle was too tense, every fiber too rigid. There was no position I could get comfortable in.

With a loud sigh I stood to get a better view of the monitor.

"The comp...er...hard...min dawn...," Clarence said in a soft voice and pointed at a folder on his screen.

"You don't have to whisper on my account." I folded my arms and fell against the radiator, which burned hot enough to singe the hairs off my legs, but I welcomed the pain. "If there's anything I need to know, you've got to tell me."

I was wet, cold, and pissed. What the hell did they want from me? A song and a dance?

Eli nodded at Clarence. "Go on."

"I have nothing else on the killings yet." Clarence sharpened his voice. "As for the company *Hard and Sweet*, it wasn't as easy to trace as you'd think. Had to call in a favor I was hoping to save for a rainy day."

Eli shook a couple of drops from his hair onto Clarence's shoulder.

"I take your point." Clarence brushed the water off his sweater and opened the folder. "Anyway. Max Hoffmann, two Ns, was merely the face of the company. The real owners are a couple of shell companies, one of which belongs to Johannes Danziger. Another German name. Makes sense, right?"

"Danzig is the German word for Gdansk." I pushed off the radiator. "Are you telling me..."

"Jack's short for John, as in Johannes, right?" Eli stared.

"Shit." I kicked the printer next to me, causing a plastic side flap to fall open. "I knew he seemed way too interested in what we were doing."

"But this?" Eli thudded his fist against the back of Clarence's chair. "Fuck."

Clarence had enough sense not to complain.

Eli had his hands rolled into tight fists, his nostrils flared. "That..."

"Save your anger for that lying son of a bitch." I moved toward the door. "Come on."

A few minutes later, we tore down the streets in my Volvo. The rain had come back with a vengeance, drenching me all over again, but for once, I didn't care.

"Come on, man." I gestured at a guy who was crossing the road.

The sun hadn't risen yet and the rain kept on coming, so why did this dude stroll like it was a sunny afternoon?

"If you didn't want to get wet, you should have stayed in bed," I mumbled, even though my quiet reproach wouldn't make the guy walk any faster.

"You're so repressed." Eli leaned over and slammed the horn repeatedly.

The man shouted something we couldn't hear and hastened to the other side. I accelerated. My wheels splashed the poor sod with water.

Unsurprisingly, he turned back around—and I flipped him off.

"Attaboy." Eli sounded smug.

I gave one of those could-mean-anything chuckles.

"I thought I'd scared Hoffmann shitless when I roughed him up." I crossed the lights at a very dark shade of amber, but nothing save for a wall would slow me. With two hours left before Parker woke, time was precious. Once again, I was close to answers, but this time, I'd allow no more hiccups.

"Yeah, I know." Eli slapped around for something and then hooked his fingers into the handle above the door.

"But what if Hoffmann wanted protection against Jack and not me?" The smudgy illumination of a lamppost fell on a newspaper delivery truck. I swerved and growled. "And we led the demon straight to him."

"To be fair, Jack led himself to Hoffmann." Eli moved his head forward to catch my eye. "But if Hoffmann's murders were a sick hobby and not connected to his business, what's Jack's angle? Why would Hoffmann be afraid of him?"

"Especially since they were, or had been, in a relationship."

He made a weird noise as I cornered into the road that led toward the darker part of town. "Hoffmann was way out of Jack's league."

A brown sedan crawled ahead of me. What was everyone doing up this early?

"You think Hoffmann was hot, too?" I turned on my blinker to overtake the car.

"AF. Don't you?"

A second vehicle came toward us in the other lane, saving me from having to answer. I pushed the gas, zoomed past Grandfather Slow, and pulled back into our lane with inches to spare.

The Volvo skidded. Its rear wheels wobbled and hurled us toward the sidewalk. I clipped the curb then counter-steered.

"The tires are on the temperamental side today." I made an ambiguous sound to demonstrate my disappointment with my vehicle's performance.

"Um, sure. It's the car's fault." Eli's one hand still clung to the handle while his other clawed at his headrest.

Eli drove a top-range car, so he probably had no idea how normal cars handled in urban environments. Always unpredictable.

Jack's house came up on our right, and I swiftly maneuvered the Volvo into position parallel—or parallel enough—to the curb.

This part of town was still asleep. None of the windows were lit, although that would change soon, when daylight came and people started their weekday routines all over again.

I shut down the engine and punched the release button for the seatbelt. "Please let me hit him."

Eli didn't move.

"What?" I glared. "I know, I know. No killing before we have answers. Just let me maim him. A little." I measured half an inch between my thumb and index finger. "He'll tell us why he was working with a murderer once I'm done with him."

"No, it's not that." Eli looked pale. Paler than usual.

Shit, maybe he was getting hungry. Bad timing, though. He'd just have to suck it.

Pun not intended.

"Coming?" I ripped the door open and slid out of the driver's seat.

Eli made an odd noise, like a failed burp, and got out of the car. "Maybe I should drive on the way back."

"Maybe you should have used your own car." I pointed my thumb at the Volvo. "My ride, my rules."

"Fine." After another dazed second, Eli gestured for me to move. "Okay. Let's get him."

The rain had finally washed away the blood. The heap of bodies was gone, too, and yet no police cordons marked the area as a crime scene. The IEA's clean-up crew had acted fast.

I made a beeline for the rear of the building where Jack had oh-so-innocently opened the door to us a couple of hours ago.

"Jack?" I knocked politely, so as not to tip him off.

Eli leaned against the door and studied me.

"What?" I knocked again, louder now.

"You're cute when you're angry."

"This really isn't the time." Still, the heat rose, and with it, a smile. "But thanks."

The door finally opened.

"Hey, guys. You've come back." Jack, or Johannes, placed his hand high up on the doorframe and playfully crossed his legs. "Have you changed your mind about—"

At long last, my fist made contact with bone as I crunched it into his face.

Jack went sprawling on his back inside his sparsely lit hall.

"Hell." He raised his hands. "What's that for?"

I kicked him in the knee. "For being a lying piece of shit."

A pair of blue running pants hugged every unsightly roll of fat, but his fashion choice didn't surprise since he probably hadn't expected to see us again.

"Stop it. What are you doing?" Jack's pitch scaled up.

Eli placed his hands on my waist to slip past me. He landed a kick himself under Jack's ribs, then dragged him up by his collar. "Jack Gdansk, or Johannes Danziger, you're under arrest. You're strongly encouraged to spill your guts and beg for leniency because the IEA takes no prisoners. Do you understand?"

This was no human cop show, and Jack should not expect the same—or any—rights as those fine folks on CSI.

"Shit." Jack glared at Eli. "How did you find out?"

"Paperwork. You can hide your business affiliations behind as many corporations as you like. The red tape's gonna give you away every time." Eli pushed his prisoner out of the hall into the darkness.

"How much do you know?" Jack dropped his head.

His subdued manner didn't fool me. He was fishing, trying to save his ass. Unfortunately for him, I was sick of not being told the truth.

"Enough to take you in." Eli yanked on Jack's collar. "You wanna take a look around inside, Ali?"

Eli's thought process was clear. We needed hard proof, print copies, and receipts. Besides, a second or two to calm down would do me good.

"I'm on it." I rushed inside and turned Jack's small apartment upside down.

His kitchen was a mess, and the bedroom smelled of something acrid. Urine maybe, or pickled onions. The living room was furnished bare-bones style. Just above the TV set hung a watercolor in the same picture frame as the one I'd discovered at Hoffmann's house. The crisscrossing lines in the metal appeared to be identical to the ones guarding the sandman's documents.

Demons just loved hiding their shit with guards, it seemed.

I climbed onto a chair, blocked the flow of magic with my thumb, and a box took form next to the TV set.

Bingo. Look at me pulling a Sherlock Holmes without Eli to hold my hand.

I pried the lid off.

A handful of tiny black boxes with short cables lay on top, and I pocketed one to show to Eli, but what really interested me was the documents. The papers inside contained tables, times of day, and graphs. The topmost paper showed Heidi's name and today's—or rather, yesterday's—date.

My legs nearly fell away from underneath me. Heidi's death hadn't been accidental. She hadn't spotted a crime by accident either, nor was this one of Lathan's revenge acts aimed at Ivy. Heidi's passing had been a part of something larger. Something more sinister.

Dammit.

Up to this point, I hadn't much considered the other victims. Heidi had been my sole focus. But seeing the kids' names unlocked something in me. They all had loved ones feeling bereft, needing answers. How many more would Jack and Hoffmann have killed if we hadn't stopped them?

I knew nothing of Hoffmann, but my image of Jack didn't tie in with the evidence in my hand. His cruelty had struck me as bitchiness rather than the stone-hearted malice of a psychopath. How had I not seen through his façade? My lie detector nose picked up spoken lies with almost a hundred percent reliability, but diverting questions and non-verbal cues wouldn't tip me off. Still, it took a slick mind to get one over on me.

After a final look around, I picked up the bunch of keys from a side table in the hallway and locked the door behind me. Eli might want to search the place later, after we'd stashed the lying asshole at the IEA's HQ.

Out on the street, puddles were no longer puddles. They'd connected into an intricate system of streams and lakes. My pants, socks, shirt, and jacket were drenched, and the water weight turned every step into a test of strength. Yet for the second time this night, I saw a light at the end of the tunnel. We were minutes away from an explanation for why Heidi had to die. Why all those kids had to die.

Eli sat in the backseat next to a bruised Jack. Somewhere between the apartment and my Volvo, Eli had softened him up. I was cool with anything that would get him to talk.

I drove back to the IEA, making sure to give Eli a smoother ride than before. Concentrating on the road and the acceleration under my feet seemed safer for all of us than obsessing over my failure to spot Jack's deception.

We had our murderer—again—but what had become clear was that I made for a lousy investigator. Jack, Lathan, Hoffmann, Heidi —I still hadn't spotted the common denominator.

I once again parked in the spot nearest the entrance. Eli pushed Jack out of the car and followed him out. I sat for a second longer, then climbed out after them and stretched my back. Eli nudged Jack along through the parking lot and past the scanner and the door into the hallway. Clarence and a woman in a lab coat—Mina, the medical examiner, I assumed—had squeezed into a doorframe. Their hard and unyielding expressions shielded their faces against the emotions that had most likely been stirred by the demon's arrest.

While Eli continued walking, I handed the geek duo the papers I'd stowed inside my jacket pocket.

"Maybe you can make sense out of them. They appear to be test results of something." I singled out the top sheet. "This one has Heidi's name on it."

"We'll do our best," Clarence said.

He and Mina took one last look at our prisoner and set off with the documents, while I hurried after Eli. His next performance was one I didn't want to miss. This was his hour of triumph. Soon, the director and everyone at the IEA who might have doubted him would have to eat crow.

Jack was guilty—we only needed to discern of what.

We stashed him inside the interrogation room behind an unmarked door. Eli tied chains around his arms and feet and followed me back out into the corridor.

"Jack's connected to the murders," I burst out. "I found a chart with Heidi's name on it. Clarence has it."

Eli gave a short whistle. "Shit. Are you okay?"

"Me? Of course. Jack can connect the dots. Make sense of it all. Let's not forget, I can present Parker with Hoffmann's accomplice."

"Does that mean you won't have to go rogue?"

I pulled back my shoulders. "I hope so."

But mainly, finally, my process of grieving could begin. I'd been holding it in for so long, my arms and neck had started to burn, and I couldn't remember the last time I took an unfettered breath.

"Then let's get this done." Eli steeled his gaze.

I followed him back through the unmarked door and closed it behind me.

CHAPTER TEN

The interrogation room had all the charm of a meat locker. A single door set inside four brushed-metal walls. No mirrors. One digital tape recorder, which Eli claimed was his own. The IEA didn't strike me as an organization that worried about evidence, or indeed about court cases, though. Rather, dents in the concrete floor and dark stains under a table leg told of bloody encounters that no judge or jury would ever get to hear about.

Jack sat chained on one side of the table, Eli on a chair opposite him. A third chair stood next to Eli, placed there for me. We'd deposited my raincoat and Eli's jacket on it for now, since my pants clung in places that made sitting uncomfortable.

What a strange night. Over the past few hours, my typically ordered existence had undergone moments of hot and cold, of energy and calm, of ups and downs. Our hunt for Heidi's killer had been less than methodical, but maybe that was how it was meant to be. Death wasn't neat. It was painful and messy.

I leaned against the wall by the door, rallying my reserves for the grand finale—the answers to all our questions.

"Jack." Eli shook his head. "Or do you prefer Johannes?"

He pronounced the name like a German soldier shouting an order.

"Call me Jack." The demon smiled, while his eyes flitted around the room. "I'm American."

"You said Max Hoffmann was a sandman." Eli rotated the microphone toward Jack. "What else can you tell us about him?"

"He was a nice guy." Jack dreamily waved his hand in the air. "Hot. Well, you saw him yourself. He liked sunsets and being tickled right here." He moved his tied hands to behind his ear.

"So you and he were in a relationship?" Eli didn't seem fazed by Jack's lack of respect.

"Yes."

"Why?"

Jack's mouth opened. Not a word came out.

"Hoffmann was, as we all agree, *hot*." Eli shrugged. "You are not. I'm not seeing any positive personality traits either, so why would he be in a relationship with *you*?"

"You're mean." Jack kicked the table, his face sullen.

"If anything..." Eli leaned forward. "I bet you never had a relationship with anyone. Are you still a virgin, Jack?"

Ouch, that must have stung. Rejection was tough for most of us, but for Jack, a guy with a genuine crush on Eli, that suggestion had to be a slap in the face.

"Why are doing this?" Jack's eyes widened into puppy eyes. "I thought we were friends."

"Friends?" Eli blew with laughter. "Us?"

"Shut up." Jack strained against his chains. "Shut up. Shut up."

"As I said." Eli chuckled again. "Hoffmann was way out of your league, and you're as poor as a church rat. You're a bottom feeder."

"I don't know why you're saying these things." Jack shifted in his chair. "I've done nothing wrong."

The smell of his lie said otherwise.

"Hoffmann owned *Hard and Sweet*." Eli took the sandman's

papers from his jacket pocket and tapped on the thin stack. "He was your boss."

"Yes. Exactly." Jack placed his cuffed hands flat on the table. "And he was mean. He killed people. You said so yourself."

"Right." Eli waved him off. "I guess it makes sense. What were you then? The janitor?"

I gave a forced laugh. "More likely, the cleaning lady."

Jack stopped shifting in his seat, his eyes narrowed.

"His doormat." Eli smiled. "He let Hoffmann walk all over him and was grateful for it."

"Don't." Jack's voice held a sudden edge.

"Why not?" Eli spread his arms wide. "Hey, if I kick you, are you going to roll onto your back for me too?"

For better or worse, the vampire had a way at provoking a reaction.

Jack was at his mercy. His cheeks were burning red, his eyes so narrow they barely showed any white.

"Pathetic." I flicked my fingers at him. "A demon cowering before a sandman."

"If only you knew." Jack's voice sounded pressed.

"But we do." Eli tapped the papers. "It's right here, in black and white. The sandman's done good, while the demon's left with nothing to show for his subservience. No money. No boyfriend. No spine."

"You wanna know how it was?" Jack slammed his hands on the table, his face distorted into an ugly mask. "Max was the weak one. When I told him to suck my dick, he did."

My heart beat on my tongue, behind my eyes, making the scent of his lie even stronger. I wagged my finger to tell him off. "Max dumped you."

"Nice try, though." Eli leaned forward, eager to squeeze more confessions out of his victim. "Max was the boss, you were the boot-licker."

"I'm telling you." Jack yanked his cuffed hands up. "I was in charge."

"You?" Eli blinked incredulously. "That makes no sense. Max killed Heidi—"

"I killed her." Jack drilled his thumb into his chest. "Me. I did it."

The second his admission left his mouth, his eyes twitched.

Too late. The bastard's words would forever be burned into my brain.

The wolf inside me gaged the distance between us. If I was fast enough, could I rip out his throat before Eli could intervene? But this wasn't the time. Eli still had more wounds to inflict on the bastard, no doubt. Hoffmann had returned Heidi, but it was Jack who'd taken her from me. And he would tell us how.

Christ, Heidi would have been unprepared for the horror she'd had to endure. The pack had kept her shielded from the evils of the world, and Jack was the worst kind of evil. If only I'd warned her about the cruelty out there, given her a glimpse of the real life, she wouldn't have snuck out. I'd failed her.

"So many victims." Eli wiped at an invisible spot on the table. "So many different methods. No way did you kill all of them."

"You think so? Here's where you got it wrong." Jack laughed the way a schoolgirl might on hearing a rude joke. "They were all killed the same way."

"By car." Eli counted the ways on his fingers. "By stabbing. By—"

"Poison. They all died of poison."

"Jack. Really." Eli sighed. "I've read the reports. The human medical examiners were meticulous."

"Humans are idiots. I used a poison so rare, they wouldn't think to look for it." He tapped his forehead. "And the IEA would never swoop in with their magic to involve themselves in seemingly accidental deaths. That's the genius. Max didn't have the brains to pull that off. Not him."

Man, had I been off in my assessment of him. Jack's eyes shone with an insanity that hadn't been there earlier. I was no stranger to violence and cruelty, but I'd never encountered this kind of icy triumph. The man before me had a narcissistic instability that made him look at the world only through his eyes. To him, compassion or empathy were words buried deep in a dictionary.

"Let's put aside the fact that *I* did see the pattern." Eli's lithe figure shifted, with lean muscles shaping the fall of his untailored T-shirt. "Your claims of being some powerful crime boss don't convince me."

"That's because you don't know who I am." Jack's expression darkened. "My people fear me. I answer to no one."

"Except Lathan." Eli dropped the name casually.

Jack's eyes widened for a fraction of a second, then he moved in his seat and tapped the table. "Lathan's my kinlord, and yes, he's my boss, but he isn't here. He doesn't know what's involved in building a successful organization."

I coughed to signal that Jack had avoided answering the question. My senses were honed to sniff out the smallest of fibs, but they'd been useless when confronted with his evasive truths. I wasn't going to get fooled again.

"Are you saying Lathan has nothing to do with this?" Eli shot me a grateful look. "He didn't send his people after us?"

"I sent them." Jack pointed at himself again. "Hired them in his name. Idiots didn't even know. And you had no clue either because I made sure they attacked me too."

Was hiring someone to punch you in the mouth clever or just really, really stupid? Jack was two opposite sides of a coin. The poise he showed right now were light years away from the bumbling and annoying sidekick I'd chauffeured around town all night.

Then again, why exactly was he so free with the truth? What was he after? Notoriety?

Jack cocked his head. "Of course, I thought that the threat of Lathan's wrath would have stopped your stupid investigation."

"Fat chance." Eli smiled wryly. "But let's get back to your methods. Our medical examiner's first class, so we know Heidi died of poison. I'm still struggling to believe the humans mistook poison for physical trauma."

"You don't get it." Jack lifted his chin. "I gave all of them poison. For scientific purposes, you understand, to see how they'd react. The lethal dose is different for each type of kin. Then, when the subjects of my study were about to die, I made Max finish them off. The poor devil loved proving his loyalty to me."

So, the chart with Heidi's name on it had been a progress report. I tensed and released the muscles in my arms repeatedly, but the relief I'd hoped for didn't set in. Her death had been the result of an experiment. What a senseless, pitiful waste of a young life.

As Parker's second, my job description was clear: diffuse sticky situations; organize the daily running of his pack; keep the books.

I'd proven my reliability—and predictability—over and over.

But Heidi hadn't yet pitched her tent. What teenager had? She'd still been figuring things out, including what she wanted from the future and who she was.

Jack took that from her.

"I admit, everything went wrong when I picked up the shifter kid." Jack bit his bottom lip and peered at me. "Max was scared of your kind. Can you believe that? Pussy told me he was done with me and my work and ran off." He shook his head. "Then the werewolf bitch died. Not my day, I tell you."

I pressed my palms flat against the metal wall, pushing as hard as my tired limbs allowed. Only a few more minutes of patience, then Jack would have told us everything. He was on a roll. To him, this wasn't a confession. It was a bragging session.

"You see, I'd concentrated the poison so it's excruciating and fatal every time but doesn't kill too soon." Jack slanted toward Eli as if they were old friends. "Even the troll kid, the fattest we could find, took two days to die with only one dose. Everything was going well."

"Then came the werewolf," Eli said.

"Yeah. I miscalculated." Jack sat back with a shrug. "At that point, my tests had been completed. The experiment was over, but I was curious. Werewolves seemed more resilient than most kin. If I was a betting man, I'd have put the girl's survival at three days, not a few hours."

"But she died quickly. How did Max end up with her body?"

"I got my guys to pick him up and reminded him that no one left me. No one." Jack swished his hand through the air. "Couldn't wait to make it up to me after that. At least that's what I thought. Promised he was gonna take care of the body. Obviously, I thought he was going to cut her up, feed her to the sharks, or something. Not for a minute did I suspect he'd take her home. When I saw the photo, I knew he'd done it deliberately."

"Good for him." Eli clicked his tongue in fake cheer. "Your mistake was telling us where to find him when we came knocking. That was downright stupid."

"What choice did I have?" Jack attempted a wide gesture, but the chains got in the way. "You came along with the walking lie detector here, so I couldn't just lie my way out of the situation."

I focused my gaze on the seams joining the large metal plates into the wall on the far end of the room, but the internal décor made a poor distraction for the revulsion crawling up my stomach lining. Jack's personality didn't just come with holes, it was a dark, stinking abyss by itself.

"A risky move to accompany us." Eli crossed his arms. "You'd have been better off getting the hell out of Silverton."

"A calculated risk. I thought Ali would kill him for sure the moment he saw him." He jerked his chin toward me. "Max tried to set me up. I merely returned the favor."

"If Heidi wasn't part of your experiment, why risk the wrath of the werewolves in the first place?" I asked.

"That's what I'm saying. Without Max's act of rebellion, there would have been no risk. Bitch was a werewolf, and there was no danger the IEA would get their hands on her body. She'd have died of an overdose or fallen off a bridge, and you furballs would have done away with her remains in private. It's the way you operate." Jack stared at me. "Usually."

He was right. Werewolves were predictable. Clearly, that wasn't always a good thing. If Eli hadn't coaxed, or rather, bribed me to swim against the stream this once, we might never have found the killer.

I flexed my biceps and deltoids, another sign my wolf was preparing to attack. "Kidnapping, let alone killing, one of us is a declaration of war."

"Smell the coffee, sunshine." Jack's expression deformed into a toothy grin. "The change is coming. Can't you feel it? You shifters are close to the end and you don't even know it."

"What are you talking about?" I tilted my head, trying to fit his words into the conversation. Despite many challenges, werewolf numbers had remained stable over the past decade.

"You're getting your war, furball, and it's going to be bloody. Your pack's isolated from everyone else. From kin, and even from your own kind. No one gives a shit about you, and no one's coming to your aid."

My wolf was about to launch at him, but a single look from Eli kept me glued to the spot. He was right. This doom-and-gloom talk was nothing new. Kinlords had been trying to break free and destroy our world for decades, and they'd continue to do so. Besides, for now, Jack was talking. I might not like what he was saying, but with every word, the picture sharpened.

"Okay, let me get this straight." Eli knocked on the table to draw Jack's focus. "You feed a bitter, foul-tasting poison to a member of each race without their knowledge. Why kids, by the way?"

Jack dropped his gaze. "Why not?"

Was he skirting the truth again? Nothing avoided answers more effectively than asking another question.

"Next, you tell Max, who's apparently under your thrall, to kill your young victims during everyday activities like playing football or while on their way home from school before the poison takes hold completely." Eli ran his hand through his hair. "I gotta tell ya, Jack. I admire your creativity."

Jack gave two thumbs-up. "Told you. Total genius."

"To come up with that much bullshit." Eli slammed his fist on the table with such speed, even my spine shot straight.

"Hey." Jack ducked away but was back to full insanity a few seconds later. "I told you nothing but the truth. Ask him."

He pointed at me.

He was right, as far as I could say, but I'd had him figured out. If he'd told us no lie, maybe we hadn't asked the right questions yet.

"Why experiment in the first place?" Eli asked. "You're not a scientist."

Jack waved him off. "Like the rest of the world, you underestimate me. Every day, I—"

The door opened, and Vanguard popped his head in. He stared at Jack, who stared back, eyebrows raised. "What's going on?"

"Director Vance." Jack squinted. "Don't you have better things to do than hang out at the office at night?"

"I work when my staff works." Vanguard's grim expression switched into an arrogant one. "What is this? Why's he here?"

"I invited him." Eli pointed between the two men. "Director, meet our local Serial Killer."

"I see." Vanguard frowned at me, then regarded Eli with a superior look. "Come see me when you're done here. Both of you."

He seemed highly irritated that Eli's hunch had paid off, and we even had the killer in custody to boot.

"Sure thing." Eli audibly ground his teeth.

Vanguard left the room, and we fixated back on Jack, who was trying unsuccessfully to cross his bound arms.

"Let's get back to your fairytale." Eli briefly puffed his cheeks. "Poisons? A criminal mastermind? Maybe. You, a scientist, experimenting on people? Come on, dude. Tell us the truth."

"You're right." Jack bit his bottom lip. "I was kidding. I didn't do a thing, and you can't prove otherwise."

The director's ill-timed interruption had broken the flow of his confession. Jack hadn't shown much respect for Lathan earlier, so coming face-to-face with Vanguard, Lathan's representative in our world, probably didn't bode well for his future.

As if he'd live long enough to be killed by Vanguard. My pack would turn him to chow the minute I brought him home with me. But we still had much to learn before then.

"Eli." I beckoned the vampire toward me with a jerk of the head.

He approached.

"Can you glamour him?" I whispered.

"I can try, but demons aren't always susceptible." Eli held his face close to my ear.

His breath swept over the hollow of my neck, giving me chills, while the wolf inside me practically rolled onto its back.

"If you can't glamour him, maybe it's time to give him to my pack, and we'll beat the rest out of him." I inched closer, inhaling his scent into me.

His shower gel or deodorant had been washed away by the rain, and what remained, his essence, blew through me and jolted my balls. Allowing myself to be near him wasn't smart. We had no future. I'd end up being hurt again. And while my head had no problem getting that, my body and heart had their own ideas.

"It's a deal." He let the warmth from his mouth dance across my skin. "After all, I've heard your pack's pretty good at it."

I didn't dare move, didn't dare break the spell he'd laid on me, but only a second later, Eli walked away.

"Right, Jack." He sat back in his chair. "Tell me about this shipment to Lawton's Bridge."

"That's none—" Jack blinked. Jerked his head. "What shipment?"

"He's playing coy again." I squinted to see if the demon showed any signs of having been glamoured yet.

"Yes." Eli took a deep breath and refocused on Jack. "The shipment."

"To Alethia?" Jack's eyes glazed over. "What about it?"

"Much demand for candy bars in Alethia, or are you using your company as a front for other goods? Slaves? Drugs, maybe?" Eli shifted in his seat as if preparing for a revelation. "If we were to raid the truck you hired, what would we find?"

"Just..." Jack's eyes darted around the room, then he leaned back and shrugged.

Whatever trance Jack had been under, it was gone. Still, he'd admitted to knowing about the IEA's super-secret portal.

"Listen, guys." His affable smile made my spine crawl. "The day-to-day was really Max's thing. I had little to do with that side of the business."

"Seriously, dude?" I flared my nostrils. "I know you're lying."

'Sorry,' Eli mouthed.

I shrugged. It made little difference to me. Glamour might not work on the demon, but good old violence would.

"Not lying." Jack leaned back and crossed his legs, making the chain that tied him to the chair rattle. "And who's killing people? Listen. Before, you know, I was only talking hypotheticals. As I said, I never did anything."

I slammed the metal wall behind me, making Jack flinch. Suddenly he plays stupid? Not on my watch.

"We have your confession right there." I gestured at Eli's recorder.

"So what?"

"You're right." Eli's voice went subarctic. "No judge is ever going to hear it. I think it's better if I hand you over to the werewolves with a bow. An actual bow, tied to your ugly face. Red or pink? I think pink's totally your color. What do you think, Ali?"

"Pink will really impress my pack. Besides, red would disappear under the blood he's going to spill."

"Never," Jack spat. "Lathan would never allow it. I'm gonna walk out of here, and there's nothing you can do about it."

"What is it?" I asked. "Is Lathan an idiot too stupid to be worth your time, or do you in fact work for him?"

"All I'm saying is I'm an innocent demon, and he'd never allow you to hand me off to a pack of dirty furballs."

That explained his willingness to talk. Lucky for us, because his reality looked entirely different.

"You think the demon kinlord cares about you that much?" I laughed. "Hell, he's sitting pretty in Alethia and won't lift a finger for a weasel like you."

"We'll see." Jack raised his eyebrows, feigning ambivalence, but he'd started plucking at his bottom lip again.

"If Lathan was involved in your scheme, protecting you would be tantamount to a confession," I said, offering a grim smile. "He wouldn't risk it. And if you pulled this off without his permission, as you seemed to imply, he'd be furious you dragged him into this mess. In that case, he'd gladly hand you over. Either way, you lose."

"I don't know what you're talking about." Jack was back to being a sulky teenager.

Dammit. Eli had done a great job playing on Jack's vanity, but we'd hit a roadblock.

"Let me put it another way." I pushed off the wall and crossed over to get in his face. "If your amnesia continues, we'll tell everyone that you killed kids of different kin because you were hell-bent on starting a war with every single race, and you did so in

Lathan's name. His fellow kinlords in Alethia would have many questions for him."

"Mehmet sure would," Eli said.

"Yes, and the fae, the trolls, the satyrs, and all the others." I tapped his chest with every word. "Lathan would not be thrilled to come under fire from all sides. No, he has no interest in saving you."

"Nice." Eli chuckled. "You should ride along on all my cases, dude."

A great career choice once Parker demoted me. At least it came with a perk in the form of one hell of a hot guy.

"Let's give him time to mull things over." Eli got up and knocked on the table. "If you don't feel like talking when I return, we're gonna invite you back to his place. It's what you've been after all night anyway. Right?" He forcefully patted the demon's cheek. "Lucky boy."

We left the room. The second the door fell into the lock, I leaned my frame against the white-washed wall, taking a much needed breather. My job was done. Jack was in custody, and I had answers. All that remained was to avenge Heidi's death, but that would be Parker's privilege. His claim as her alpha superseded mine. Good thing he didn't hold back when he got angry. Jack would suffer extensively before taking his dying breath.

As for me, once again, the notion of achieving closure remained a specter, hanging over my head, out of reach. I didn't regret the actions I'd taken tonight, but there was more I could have done when Heidi had still been alive. Teenage girls had never been an interest of mine, but I could have tried to understand her better. Build bridges. What music did she even listen to? What movies excited her? Heidi had been the youngest among us, and a girl to boot. Trapped in a pack of mainly testosterone-driven males, her feelings of loneliness must have been immense.

Christ, here I was, having brilliant insights way too late.

"Are you all right?" Eli rested beside me, probably as exhausted as I was, although he didn't show any overt signs of his batteries running out. "You're quiet. More so than usual, I mean."

"I was thinking, next week, I might visit Keely's pack of females. They don't trust males in general, but my being gay should make them feel safe."

"Okay, master of segues." Eli nudged me with his shoulder. "Any particular reason?"

"I thought if I told them about Heidi, and about the mistakes I've made raising her, they might, in turn, give me a glimpse into their lives. You know, show me how Heidi would have spent her days." I tapped my knuckles against the wall, soaking in the pain. "I know it makes no sense. She's gone. I just—"

"No, I get it. One of my colleagues died two weeks into my new job. For months I obsessed about finding out everything I could about the guy."

"Why do we do crazy shit like that?"

"Dunno. To ease the pain? Maybe understanding the ones we lose is the only way to get closure." Eli expelled a long sigh. "Are you ready to face Vanguard? You don't have to come. He's not your boss."

I pushed off the wall and started walking, knowing he'd follow. "I'll come. You have my back, I have yours. That's what partners do."

CHAPTER ELEVEN

At the first junction, Eli took the lead, and we moved through the snaking corridors until I'd lost my bearing. A few doors stood open along the way. By appearances, most rooms served for storage rather than as offices. Was the might of the IEA an illusion? Was the building an empty husk? Then again, this was only one floor out of several, not counting the basement, and it was still the middle of the night—or rather, early morning. By day, these halls might be teeming with activity.

Eli knocked on an unmarked door.

"Come," Vanguard yelled.

He acknowledged us with a curt nod without lifting his gaze off the computer screen in front of him.

That dude deserved an ass-whooping, but it probably wouldn't be a good idea for me to initiate a war with the IEA. It might undo all the good I'd done helping to apprehend Heidi's killer.

"Tell me about Jack." The director shifted his chair to the left, so he could see past his computer, and leaned back with his fingers locked behind his head.

"Our former snitch has moved up the ranks since you first recruited him." Eli's dig at his boss filled a spiteful hole in my chest.

The vampire stood with his hands in his pockets, his shoulders back. Not an ounce of deference about him. Vanguard really was an unpleasant character, and Eli was too good at his job to put up with his crap.

"He admitted to poisoning the victims and orchestrating the murders of all kin children except the werewolf kid, whose death he's solely responsible for." Eli pointed his jaw at me. "I'm prepared to hand him to the werewolves as soon as we leave."

"So. Your hunch was right." Vanguard regarded Eli coolly. "Very well. But Jack stays here."

"Director?" Eli's gruff voice of disbelief filled the room.

"All due respect, but that's unacceptable." I approached the desk. "Heidi was one of ours. The responsible party's sitting in your interrogation room. He's admitted to his crime, so unless you're prepared to piss off werewolves all over the country..."

"I don't need to justify myself to you." Vanguard dropped his arms and straightened.

Eli stood calm, unmoving. "Director."

"Jack's a demon, so his fate will be decided by the demon kinlord." Vanguard kept Eli in his sight. "Those are the rules."

"Lathan might be involved in this." I pounded my fist on his desk.

"That's an outrageous accusation." The director slowly raised his eyebrows. "The IEA operates on the indulgence of the seven kinlords. Before the kinlords entered Alethia, they formed our agency to represent their interests here in this realm. To this day, they dictate our agenda. If I hand a demon over to outsiders without informing his kinlord first, the consequences for our organization would be immeasurable."

The director's position as a go-between had to suck, sure. With all the privileges of his position came the unenviable task of keeping peace between kin in our world and between the kinlords within Alethia. But his rules weren't mine.

Still, I was prepared to give him a chance to do right by my pack—as long as I ended up with Jack in my possession. Pink bow optional.

"Inform Lathan, if you have to." I gave a nod of permission. "For your sake, I hope he makes the right decision."

"Don't threaten me." The director ran his hand over his crew cut. "But between us, Lathan has no interest in pissing off your pack."

"Right." I countered his lie with a doubting glower but suppressed the growl forming in my throat. "Anyway. The ball's in your court."

"As it has always been." Vanguard met my stare with his own, and then shooed us out of his room. "Now go. Let me do my job."

Eli marched out of the room and down the hallway. Stopped. Punched a wall. Continued marching.

The wall's paint crumbled around a tear at the impact site.

I felt his pain, more so since I was running out of time, but I'd have my hand on the prize one way or another. Parker would forgive my infractions, at least most of them, once he understood what I'd achieved. What *we'd* achieved, Eli and I.

"It's a delay. Don't worry." In the middle of a sort of break room, I stood behind Eli and put my hand on his shoulder. "The director's promise was made without deceit. What's another half hour? Right?"

My breathing intensified, a sound he couldn't possibly miss. Maybe he'd attribute it to the excitement of the moment and not to the idea I'd sought contact with him.

Eli didn't turn, but he didn't run away from my touch either. "I gave you my word that you'd have closure. The entire pack, I mean."

"We will. Okay?" Emboldened, I tightened my grip. "You've come through for me. For us. I'll still face punishment, but the answers together with Jack should at least save me from exile. Thank you."

His muscles softened under my hand.

Wow. My touch had relaxed his body. I suppressed the smile threatening to break on my face.

"You're welcome." He rolled his eyes. "Of course, I only worked so hard to find the killer because I know you wouldn't survive as a rogue without my help."

"Oh, you think so, do you?"

"Got a minute, boss?" Clarence approached, holding a thin stack of documents.

I quickly dropped my arm and headed to the huge coffee-making contraption that took up an entire table.

"Mind if I do?" I grabbed a cup and waved it through the air.

"Only if you get me one, too." Eli turned his focus to Clarence. "What is it?"

"We looked through the reports Ali gave us. Mina says they're progress reports on the same poison that killed the werewolf girl."

I breathed hard but kept my shit together, arranging two cups by the nozzle by way of distraction.

"Heidi, you mean." Eli sounded grim.

I shot him a grateful look.

"Heidi, right. Sorry." Clarence rustled the papers. "The charts track the victims' health in minute detail. Feelings of sickness, vomiting, diarrhea... All written by the same hand, so it doesn't appear Jack had help. Heidi was hit the hardest. She never stood a chance."

Why hadn't Jack picked on me to try out his poison? Why did it have to be the youngest in our pack? The one with the brightest future?

I snapped the nozzle back and bit my lip. Gadgets weren't my forte, and the gleaming coffee machine with its levers and buttons confused the hell out of me. Abandoning the cups for a moment, I turned to concentrate on their conversation instead.

"He, Jack I mean, poisoned them." Clarence took a jagged breath. "All of them. And he observed them. He must have gained their trust to do that, although it doesn't say how. When the pain moved from internal discomfort to full-blown symptoms, he had them..." Clarence crushed the paper in his large hand into a ball. "Terminated. He had them terminated. That's the word he used."

"I'm sorry." Eli patted his arm. "At least we know, right?"

The troll's outpouring of emotion seemed unusual for someone who had to deal with death a lot as part of working for the IEA, but then, the crimes had been particularly heinous.

"I guess." Clarence sniffed, and within a second was back to his composed self. "Jack administered the cucurbitacin to his first three victims over the course of a few days. Then he studied their wellbeing. He, or rather his partner 'M'—which I assume stands for Max—sometimes got very close to them."

"They were kids and too trusting." Eli scratched his ear. "Why weren't the children laid up or in the hospital?"

"It seems the pain comes in waves, so they just went about their lives at first. Jack's breakthrough occurred after victim number five. From then on, a single dose brought guaranteed death, usually after two to three days. The sheer agony of the final cramps indicated it was time for 'M' to do his thing. To terminate the victims. Only Heidi passed away almost immediately."

"That ties in with what Jack told us." I inched closer to them. "What we don't yet know is how he poisoned them. Did he spike their water?"

"No idea." Clarence held up the balled paper in his hand. "These reports only show the results, not the how."

"What about your medical examiner?" I asked. "Does she have any guesses?"

"Without an autopsy, she can't say how or when the poison was ingested. She's popped out to get breakfast, but I'll send her your way when she's back." He fixed his gaze on me. "We're not done with our investigation yet."

"Thanks, dude." Eli dismissed Clarence with another slap on his shoulder.

"I assume your machine here requires a college degree to operate?" I jerked my head toward the contraption.

"We offer a full scholarship to all our appliances, but this one dropped out halfway through its first term." Eli took off his sweater and handed it to me while untucking the white T-shirt he wore underneath. "Come on. I'll show you."

He lifted levers, filled water into one tank, and added coffee to another, offering me a prime view of his arms and back. He was lean, certainly, but also perfectly proportioned. Vampires didn't need to work out for their strength, but Eli's muscles were far more chiseled than Florian's.

"I didn't mean anything earlier." Eli studied the steaming jet of brown liquid filling the first cup. "About you having a stick up your ass. I meant, I know doing this—driving around, investigating—it's not the way werewolves would handle things."

"You weren't entirely wrong either. We do enjoy a structured schedule."

"You *are* a bit Stepford Werewolves as a group." He chuckled and gestured to the cup he'd just set down. "All of you, broad shoulders, a serious expression on your face... Basically, the same shade of vanilla."

"You're calling *me* vanilla?" I pointed my thumb at myself. "I don't know if you've noticed, but the Indonesian in the pack does stand out."

"I didn't know ethnicity was a thing for you." His voice hitched as he started filling the other cup. "Isn't life among your pack all peace, love, and pancakes?"

"Yeah, it is. Mostly." I picked up my coffee. Its heat ate into my skin, and I quickly placed it back on the table. "And yet, off-the-cuff remarks about a California tan are typically followed by guilty glances and mumbled apologies, as if the mere mention of skin tone is an insult. And when we get take-outs, I get the spicy dish, even though I didn't order it."

"That blows." He slammed a lever, and the nozzle cut off the stream. "Where are your parents? In Indonesia?"

"No, they came over to the US in the fifties. Set up a small pack near Colorado Springs. Mostly Indonesians and other Asian werewolves. My parents' outlook is very black and white."

"You're not getting on?"

"I'm gay. That's unacceptable to my family. After I came out, I continued to live with them, but for all intents and purposes, I was in exile. I had to stay in my room, eat separately from them, at least until I'd *come to my senses.*"

"Nuts." He turned to me, the look in his eyes one of unbridled curiosity. "Does who you love matter that much to them?"

"What can I say?" I briefly arched my eyebrows in a sort of shrug. "Some werewolves aren't as flexible when it comes to matters of sex as you vampires are."

"So you do remember that I practice yoga." He waved me off. "Of course you do. And your strict family background does explain your no-boxers philosophy, too. A picture is beginning to form of you, my friend."

"Excellent." I carried my cup by its rim to a table near the window.

"At least you got out of there," Eli said. "Parker's pack treats you well?"

"Sure. Over the years, Parker and I got close, and I feel more at home there than I did with my people."

"Riiight." He drew out the word as if he'd stumbled onto a key insight. "You say *more* at home. But not completely?"

"I feel at home there, I meant. My friends are there, my work. But let's not pretend I'm like them. The color of my skin, for one." I gave a smile that hopefully told him I wasn't too fussed. "Not a huge deal for them, luckily. Sometimes I think I have more of a problem with it than they do. I've never felt fully accepted anywhere. I'm not Asian-looking enough for Indonesians, nor do I speak Bahasa. I'm not a Muslim, nor a Christian. Not straight. And definitely not easygoing. So put me anywhere, and I'm the outsider."

"Yes, you're definitely looking for reasons to be a victim." Eli placed his chin in his propped-up hand and gave me his full attention. "If you ask me, there's enough variety in life to be who you want to be without feeling different. For example, what do you like? Really like, I mean?"

We sat on opposite chairs, and I pulled back my legs under me, so as not to accidentally kick him.

"Like?" I blew onto my coffee in the vain hope of cooling it. "I don't know. Football."

"Hardly makes you original." He crinkled his nose. "Tell me about yourself."

"Okay. I got my accounting degree—"

"No." He wagged his hand. "Something personal. Something nobody else knows."

"All right. I can do that. Something nobody... Okay. For me, everything tastes better with sweet soy sauce." I grinned. "Not sure if that's an Indonesian thing or not."

"Might be an Ali thing. What else?"

What did he care? I'd already shared too much with him. Being Florian's brother lent him an air of familiarity, but really, he was a stranger.

I dimmed my grin to a two-cent smile. "I'm a normal guy."

"You just told me how different you are." He puffed out his cheeks. "Fine. You're not ready to open up yet, but as I said, the night's young."

For six months, I'd been accusing Florian of being secretive. Unable to share his feelings. Here was his brother, doing the same to me. Talk about karma.

"Anyway." I mellowed my tone. "What about you? I know practically nothing about you, except you like drinking blood."

"That I do." His shoulders jerked as if suppressing a chuckle. "I assume my brother has told you about our wild days in Europe?"

"Yeah, a little. Where were you born?"

"In Denmark."

"Eli isn't a Danish name."

"My given name was Christian, but my sire renamed me Eli." He huffed. "Gino was going through a phase. My sister got a new name too, although I can't remember her original one. Too long ago."

"I didn't know that."

"It wouldn't have come up because Florian got to keep *his* name." The bite in his words was back.

"What is it with you two?" I leaned forward. "You're like lightning rods for each other, but aren't you supposed to be brothers?"

"That's the idea." Eli's look drifted to the window facing the dark parking lot, where raindrops fell to the ground in thick, white strings. "I don't think he cares for me."

"You're wrong. He makes fun of you behind your back, sure, but the fact that he mentions you as often as he does speaks volumes."

"Maybe. He was the favorite, you know? The baby. When he messed up, it was, 'Oh, leave him alone.' If I did something wrong, it was, 'You must set a better example for your brother.'"

"That's not Florian's fault."

"Sure, because milking his advantage so isn't him, right?"

I had little to counter that argument. Florian could be incredibly selfish and cocky, although most of that was bravado. Still, being around him was hard work.

Eli was different. He made everything easy. Even tracking down a killer.

"Look at what you've achieved in a few hours, despite all the setbacks." I kept any emotion from my tone. "And you had me to contend with, too. By the way, you could have glamoured me into helping you. But you didn't."

"I could have glamoured you into handing over Heidi's body, sure, but keeping it up all night—and by 'it' I meant the glamour." He widened his eyes in mock innocence. "That would have drained me. Then I would have had to feed off you, and that could have made things weird between us."

"Probably."

Letting him drink from me didn't sound as horrific as it should. Maybe there was something wrong with me. I couldn't make my mother happy by finding a nice werewolf girl, but what the hell was so difficult about finding a nice werewolf boy to fantasize over? Did it have to be a vampire?

We sat for a few minutes staring at our steaming cups. Aside from the two of us, the room was empty, but that would change soon. In a few hours, IEA officers would trundle into work. What would happen if I was still here then? The yellowish light from the bright ceiling lamps would shine the spotlight on me, a werewolf in their hallowed hallways.

No, all things going well, I'd be elsewhere then. The plan was to present Parker with Heidi's killer by the time he sat down for his cereal. My pack had the setup to beat the remaining answers out of Jack once he was in our custody. Later, I'd share the answers with Eli.

Better yet, I could invite him to come with me and observe. Watching violence-in-action might be an odd first date, but combined with a beer and some popcorn, I might be on to a winner.

"Jack said he enjoyed studying people." Eli spooned sugar into his coffee and stirred. "But how did he or Max observe them? Did they chase them around town on bikes? Catching their death cramps can't have been easy."

"They were kids. They're more trusting than grumpy adults. Even Heidi." I fished the small box from my pant pockets and showed it to him. "I found half a dozen of these at Jack's place. Could be cameras."

"Yeah." He turned the device over in his hands and nodded. "Why kids, though? And how did he get them to ingest a bitter poison?"

"Jack still has a lot to tell us." I drank my coffee and grimaced. "Okay, that's it. Who buys the coffee around here?"

"Mina. I should have warned you." He pushed the sugar toward me. "Here."

I added two spoonfuls and took another sip. "Better."

Eli frowned and stared at me. Then at the sugar.

"Sugar." I put the cup down. "That's how Jack masked the taste of his poison. He put it in something sweet. Heidi had a sweet tooth."

Eli's mouth moved, but he didn't join in my Eureka moment.

"What? Think I'm wrong?" Then I slapped the table. "The candy bars."

"Yeah, the candy bars." His eyes drifted to the side as they so often did, as if he was watching answers unfold before him.

"There must be records of what went into those bars," I said. "Jack and Max kept documents on everything else."

"Come on." Eli abandoned his coffee and, sweater in hand, headed out of the room. "Let's find out."

I pushed my chair flush with the table and left my cup of warming badness on it behind to follow him into Clarence's IT office.

"Did you dig into Hoffmann's company, Clarence?" Eli's tone was back to bossy again.

"Some," the troll said. "Why?"

"Can you print the finances you found?"

"I can, as far as I have them." Clarence typed away, calling up one screen full of numbers after another. "There's not much, though. Must have hidden the rest somewhere, but I'm still looking."

The printer whirred to life and spat out around twenty sheets of paper.

While I pored over the numbers, Clarence whizzed through the words on his computer screen. Eli rocked onto his toes and tapped two fingers against his thigh.

"The numbers don't make sense." I pointed at the sheets in my hand. "According to this, *Hard and Sweet* lost money on one end and poured non-existing profits back into it as investments." I waved the paper around. "This is for show, and it's not convincing either. I don't get it. If they were hoping to make a profit, they need real records. Even kin must pay taxes."

"Maybe turning a profit was never the goal." Eli nibbled his bottom lip.

"Here, they purchased the cucurbitacin." Clarence pointed at the screen. "It's such a rare poison, they saw no need to hide the invoices. Hell. They bought huge amounts of the stuff."

"Is it possible they didn't just lace a few batches with zucchini poison, but every candy bar they produced?" Eli ran his hands through his hair and paced up and down. "Because I'm getting a real bad feeling over this."

"Yeah, a lot of people might be getting sick or die." I dropped the useless documents on a stack on Clarence's desk.

"Kids." Eli gestured vaguely but with force. "A lot of *kids* will die."

"Yeah." I leaned against the radiator, drawing comfort from its warmth. "Is there a cure?"

"Mina might be able to tell us." Eli halted his steps and stared at a poster on the wall. "I should be getting in touch with my contacts. See what they know, or at least warn them."

Eli retrieved the flat, polished communication stone from his pocket and left the room.

Clarence mumbled something and turned his attention back to his computer.

Why would Jack wish to send poisoned candy bars to Alethia?

Had he realized that his research was under threat of discovery from the IEA and decided to shift the setting of his experiments to the realm of the kinlords? That would have been a bold move and undoubtedly spelled his death, if discovered.

Unless he worked for Lathan after all, who might have already set up a lab for him in his castle.

"How are you doing?" Clarence swiveled his chair around.

"I'm okay." I eyed him carefully. Had I given off signs that I was struggling emotionally? Because, sure, I was bone-tired, but the job was done. I was allowed to relax. "How are *you* doing?"

He rummaged in the pocket of his jacket that he'd draped over his backrest to retrieve a photo.

I took it from him and studied it. "That's you."

In the picture, Clarence was sitting on a park bench, beaming alongside two boys licking ice cream.

"These are my nephews. Tom, the one on the right, was one of Jack's victims, just as Heidi was."

My jaw moved before the words gushed out. "I didn't know that. I'm sorry."

"That's why I came in the middle of the night. Eli was the first to take an interest." His cheeks slackened for a moment as he quietly exhaled. "My sister didn't want to believe that anyone could have harmed Tom deliberately, but Eli's hunches are usually right."

"He's damn good at his job."

"Indeed." Clarence grabbed the photo and smiled. "You two make a good team."

I chuckled and shifted my weight to my other leg. "I didn't contribute a lot. It was mainly just him."

"He prefers working alone. Although a few times, he's partnered up with Waylon, which really ticked off the director." Clarence leaned in confidentially. "Waylon's a guardian."

He was also Ivy's mentor and teacher. "I know him."

"Yeah?" Clarence straightened at lightning speed. "What's he like? They say he can make people cry with a single glance."

Rumors about Guardians were rife with exaggeration, actively encouraged by Waylon himself. As long as people feared him, they were unlikely to attack him.

"Maybe." I made a mental note to tell Ivy. She'd get a real kick out of it. "All I know is he swears a lot, but all in all, he's a decent guy."

And extremely hot. Sadly, Waylon was also extremely straight, just one of the reasons Parker wasn't at ease with Ivy spending a lot of time in his company.

"The director can't stand Waylon any more than Eli, although he's more polite to the guardian, of course." Clarence pocketed his family picture and returned his focus to the screen.

"Makes sense. Waylon has the power to dispatch the director to Alethia. That's a fate worse than death."

"Yeah, that must be it." His shoulders twitched with silent laughter. "Although Eli could kick his ass, too."

"Hell, I'd bring the popcorn for that show."

The door opened, and Vanguard stormed in, like the proverbial devil we'd spoken of. His light blue shirt sported a large, dark patch near his collar. "Where's Dupree?"

"Eli's stepped out." My insides clenched at the idea of dealing with the demon bully without Eli's soothing presence. "Can I help?"

The faint yet distinctive smell of grass surrounded me, mingling with the scent of hot printer ink. Vanguard wouldn't be able to pick up such nuances, though. Demons generally had two talents: brute strength, and a penchant for violence. At least, that used to be my assessment. Tonight, though, Jack had proven demons were also capable of great cunning, and the director himself had to have some form of leadership skills to become head of the IEA.

"You? Help? I doubt it." Vanguard eyed me before aiming his glare at the troll. "Clarence, I need everything you've got on Jack. Tell Dupree the investigation's over."

"We're not done questioning him, but the pack will take care of that." I pushed myself off the radiator. "Thanks."

"You misunderstood. Jack's under Lathan's jurisdiction, and the kinlord's decided to protect him." Vanguard eyed me cautiously. "I had no choice but to set Jack free."

CHAPTER TWELVE

"You let Jack go?" My growl was an instinctual response, a rare showing of my wolf in front of others. "Are you crazy? He's poisoning kids."

"The decision's been made. The moment Lathan heard your pack was involved, he closed down the investigation." Vanguard added a faint smile to my injury. "He really doesn't like your pack."

"You might have earned yourself more trouble than you can handle." I shoved him with force. "We'll make sure every kin knows you helped the killer escape."

He threatened to tumble but caught his balance by holding on to Clarence's chair.

"Lathan's ruling is final." The mighty director didn't push back, but each of his words cut. "And the werewolf community isn't going to start a war with us over one guy."

Wouldn't we? In the first flush of anger, Parker would mobilize every wolf under his command, but to what effect? The magic that kept Lathan confined in Alethia was also the magic that prevented us from crossing over. Werewolves didn't even have access to a trade portal through which we could force our way in. And waging war against the IEA was just as pointless. That would be tantamount to challenging all races of kin at once.

In the end, my alpha would do nothing at all, because our self-imposed isolation hadn't bought us many friends or allies. The director was right. We were politically impotent.

"Shut it down, Clarence." Vanguard's troubled look quickly collapsed, and he pointed at the screen. "Or lose your job."

"Yes, sir." Clarence's Adam's apple leaped, but he turned off the monitor.

"Tell your friend, will you?" Vanguard walked out with his head held high.

I stood, stunned. A few minutes ago, Jack had been in my possession and I thought I'd avoided being exiled. The demon's capture was supposed to be the redemption for my failings, help me cement my position, and allow us to express our grief. Now, the killer had slipped through my fingers.

Again.

I sank into a crouch, forced my lungs not to follow my mind's tailspin.

"My contacts were of no use." Eli entered the office and cast an annoyed glance over his shoulder. "What did the director want?"

The director had conveniently broken the news when Eli was out of earshot. What a coward.

"Hey, Ali." He approached and bent to level his gaze with mine. "What's wrong?"

I shook my head, not yet ready to talk. It took all my willpower to stand up again.

"Vanguard shut down the investigation and asked for the evidence we've collected." Clarence seemingly shrunk in his seat. "No doubt to make it disappear. Lathan told him to let Jack go."

"He did what?" Eli's eyes went darker than the swirl in my guts. He took a step to the side and ran his hand through his hair, then pointed at the computer. "Make copies of everything before you hand the files to Vanguard. Even the printouts." He tapped on the papers on Clarence's stack of documents. "Don't tell the director."

"Eli." Clarence pleaded with his eyes.

"He'll never know." Eli smoothed his expression and his voice. "You still want justice for your nephew, don't you?"

Clarence bowed his head and booted up his computer again.

Eli paced in small circles around the room. A sort of energy enveloped him, a nervous buzz—while I couldn't even find a curse word in me. I was done. Exhausted. Parker would have my hide, then kick me out. The rules I once helped him create demanded it.

The irony wasn't lost on me.

"We'll find Jack." Eli placed a heavy hand on my shoulder so I'd meet his gaze. "And we'll deliver him to Parker today. Okay?"

The determined line of his mouth promised that everything would work out.

"It's too late." The large clock on the computer's screen showed it was six o'clock. "Jack's long gone."

I shouldn't have agreed to this madcap adventure in the first place. What made me think I was something other—something better—than plain old Ali? Eli had painted this picture of a heroic me returning to my pack with the killer's head on a platter, or maybe I'd been the creator of that particular delusion. Either way, I'd failed utterly and completely, and no apology would make up for it.

In another couple of hours, the pack's blissful routine would come crashing down. I was merely the messenger waiting to be shot.

"Do you want to put Heidi back outside your house?" Eli inhaled slowly. "Go home and pretend the night never happened? We could do that, you know."

I scoffed. "Seriously?"

"Yeah. But that's not you, is it?" He moved his hand around my neck, stopping short of pulling me into his embrace. "You don't hide from consequences."

The feel of him on my skin trembled through me.

"No. And I walked into this with my eyes wide open." I twisted from his grasp. "The mistakes are my own. Working with you, with the IEA, that was my first one."

"Kick me when I'm down." He tensed through his whole body. His eyes were back to their original blue, but the lightness had left them. "You really feel that way?"

I was such an ass. Blaming others for my shortcomings was a dick move.

"No. Of course not." I released a sigh. "You were great. You, Clarence, Mina, you've all done what you could for Heidi, and I'm glad I was a part of it. I'm just, God, I'm so monumentally fucked."

"And not in a good way." Eli's expression was quickly back to only semi-serious. "Sorry."

That guy had no off switch, and I'd never appreciated his inappropriate weirdness more.

"Don't apologize. I needed perspective." I laughed a sort of lived-in laugh that tumbled haltingly from my throat. "Okay. Say we're going after Jack—again. He's not going to be at home."

"No, but we still have more than an hour left to find him." A high-powered, confident grin blew across Eli's face. "Don't count us out. We got the killer, twice, already. And next time, it's going to stick. Rule one: we won't involve the IEA."

Jack had most likely hightailed it out of Silverton the moment Vanguard let him go. I would have. Eli's pep talk didn't change that. But even working a dead end was better than going home to Parker's disappointment and grief. It was my job to make his life easier, and I'd failed him. I'd certainly failed Heidi.

Clarence slid flash drives and sheets of paper into a plastic bag and handed it to Eli. "Promise me that monster won't walk away from this."

"He won't." Eli placed his hand on the troll's shoulder. "By the way, did you look into Jack's past at all? Did he have a degree? Family? Assets?"

"He didn't finish high school, even though he was a good student. Fifteen years ago, he opened a shop selling high-end watches, although rumor had it his business was a front for other activities. Trafficking people and narcotics. But nothing ever stuck."

"That's probably when Vanguard recruited him as an informant for you." I gave a thumbs-up. "Smart move."

"Jack has family in Alethia, but none in Oldworld." Clarence focused on me. "Oldworld is *this* realm."

"I know." I shared a patient smile. "We werewolves haven't quite lost contact with kin life yet."

"Anyway, other than that, he's got a clean record." Clarence tapped a few keys on his keyboard without paying attention to the changing windows on his screen. "As hard as it is to believe."

"Not so hard considering he enjoys Lathan's protection. Thanks, Clarence. Wish us luck." Eli turned to look at me.

I nodded, and he marched out of the room. I followed behind, nearly slipping on a wet patch in the hallway, and caught up with Eli within a few steps. "Where are we going?"

"To pick up your girl. If we don't, the director might keep her as evidence, too."

Good point. There was a reason I'd never challenged Parker for alpha-hood. Aside from being his friend, I wasn't made for the cutthroat thinking the position demanded. Ruthlessness was an admirable talent, and my kind had it in spades. It kept us alive. It made us feel free.

I just never had the stomach for it myself.

Eli did. More so than any wolf I knew. And he was fearless when it came to dishing it out.

We entered the cold morgue full of clean, biting smells. My vision was oddly unfocused, my head congested. I needed coffee and a good night's sleep, but I wouldn't rest until I had something to show for our pains.

"I left my coat in interrogation." I crossed my arms against the chill.

"Forget it. Let's call it collateral damage. Let's do this before Vanguard stops us." Eli checked behind the wall of death and its many metal doors that hid the bodies from view. "Here she is."

He pulled out a gurney with a black body bag on it.

"Won't she, you know, smell?" I didn't check if it was really her. Seeing her face now, after yet another setback, might just do me in.

"No. Mina uses a special guard for her body bags. See?" He pointed at a metal plate that contained telltale intersecting grooves. "It will keep her cool for days."

I heaved Heidi onto my shoulder. After all the effort we'd put into finding answers, she was still dead. Nothing I'd done had made a difference. Not to her.

Eli walked ahead to open the doors into the parking lot, which had become one large puddle. Every step splashed dirty water onto my pant legs, yet I barely even winced.

The morning beckoned on the horizon in the form of a dark gray strip. Not so much a silver lining as it was an omen of what might lie ahead.

"Keys?" Eli beckoned.

Unable to put Heidi down, I reached around with my left hand, but I lacked the flexibility to grasp the fob.

"There are easier ways to get me into your pants," Eli whispered into my ear and slipped his fingers inside my pocket to retrieve the fob.

Heat flooded my head, but the dark would keep my reaction a secret. As for my racing heart, he'd have picked that up immediately. Keeping secrets from vampires took more commitment than I had energy for.

The headlights flashed. Eli opened the trunk and headed toward the driver's seat.

I stowed the bag gently inside the trunk, touched the end I suspected held Heidi's head, and shut the lid.

After a final glance at the building I hoped to never set foot in again, I sat beside Eli, squinting at him. "If you get to drive my car, I should get to drive yours."

"Sure. How about the next time we rob the IEA, you're the getaway driver?" He backed out of the spot and drove across the parking lot as we headed home to Custer Fields.

Seated in my sodden clothes inside my once pristine car, I let the bright signs of Silverton flash past as one long light strip. "What's our next move?"

"Go home and pore over the materials Clarence gave us. Something in them will tell us where Jack's hiding."

I nodded, too weak to stretch to an actual answer.

We'd never find Jack, of course, but it felt good trying. Would I convince Parker I'd done enough? We knew the name of the killer and what he looked like. We also knew Lathan protected him, if he wasn't even behind the whole scheme in the first place. What more did my alpha expect? What more could Rollo have achieved, or Jim, or any other wolf Parker would have sent in my place?

Eli changed lanes to avoid a large puddle. He wasn't a fast driver but a confident one, and ten minutes later, we turned into his drive. He switched off the ignition. The finality of the ride and the silence nearly made me howl. Not out of pain or loneliness, but rather to release the pressure in my stomach and chest. It had been building all night and finally reached bursting point.

But even if I wanted to, my throat wasn't built for howling. Only my wolf had that ability, and a shift in my current, fragile state could make me lose myself in my animal form.

Maybe that would be my salvation. As a wolf, I'd slink into the woods, and month after month, all the painful memories would disappear. I'd know no more hurt or betrayal, and the concept of good and evil would be meaningless.

Instead, I climbed out and took a deep, steadying breath.

CHAPTER THIRTEEN

li's home was a facsimile of my pack's in terms of size, although that was where the similarities ended. Vines curled and snaked along the outer walls unchecked, giving it an Addams-family vibe that suited the Duprees. On the other side of the road, no more than two minutes from here, the rest of my pack lay wrapped in their blankets. None of them knew what had happened. How two men had stolen Heidi's life, and how I'd allowed them to escape pack justice. A new swell of ache surged with every expelled breath.

My mission had failed due to my incompetence. Rollo wouldn't have allowed Hoffmann to jump to his death. Parker wouldn't have allowed Eli to take Jack to the IEA. Jim wouldn't have snuck out in the middle of the night. Dammit. Had I honestly thought I was Superwolf? Had Eli's words made me believe I was qualified for anything other than paperwork?

"Hey." Eli grabbed my arm. "Are you okay?"

"I'd thought I could get it done." I fumbled with my messy, soggy shirt before dropping my hands. No one noticed whether my clothes were clean or my socks were wet. No, people cared about actions, because only results mattered.

"You did what you could." Eli peered toward the pack's mansion. "They can't expect more than that."

"Doing my best is a damn low bar to set." I pressed the heel of my hand against the bruised flesh around my lip, drinking down the burn. "Jack walks, and Heidi doesn't. How is that right?"

"It's not." He pulled me close and nudged me along as he walked to his house. "I'm so sorry."

Once he'd unlocked the door, we entered a broad hallway, and Eli led me up the shadowy staircase to his quarters.

I'd visited Florian's rooms, which were located in a different wing—huge spaces that could have bunked ten men—but I'd never thought I'd venture beyond them in this strange building. Everything here seemed odd. The chill clinging to the walls, the smells, even the windows had a quirky feel with their gray frames and small size.

Eli deposited me on a lonely chair in his living room and crouched, placing his hands on the arm rests on either side of me. "What can I do? Tell me."

"Rewind time." I eyed the chrome-surround ceiling lights,

aware of every drenched inch of clothing hugging my body. "So many things I'd do differently."

"Are you scared of what Parker's going to do?"

"Yes. No." I shrugged with an indifference I didn't feel. "I've been relying on my friendship with him for too many years. He gave me a home. Prevented me from having to go rogue. Maybe he'll save me one last time, but what man can live on favors? I can't let him carry me the rest of my life. Pack rules demand my expulsion."

"Neither of us got what we wanted tonight, but regret has never solved anything. You know what has?" Eli grinned. "Alcohol."

I gave a tired laugh. "I could do with a drink."

Getting blotto seemed like a perfectly healthy alternative to lonely misery.

"That's the spirit." Eli got to his feet. "I have a six pack."

Beer wouldn't get me drunk quickly, but it was all a matter of quantity.

He rushed off, giving me a minute to myself.

Ironic, really. He was the perfect antidote to all my social ailments, wrapped in a package that appealed visually, too. This should have been a time to dazzle him with my talents and parade my strengths. Instead, the last few hours had laid bare my weaknesses.

When Eli returned, he placed six cans of beer on the floor, then rifled through his closet, from where he pulled a couple of sweaters and jeans.

"Here you go." He threw me one of each.

In the bright light, his paleness made his skin almost luminous, an indication his body wasn't pumping enough blood. Not surprising, since he'd spent hours running around in the rain.

"Get a towel and dry yourself," I ordered. "I'll make a fire."

"I'll be good once I'm dry." His smile, for once, showed a hint of uncertainty. "Don't fuss."

"I'm cold, too, and not in a mood to argue."

After a theatrical sigh, he took a quick detour into the bathroom and emerged with a couple of towels.

I cleared the ash from the fireplace, built a stash of kindling and paper, and waited for the flames to grow before placing a log on top. The comforting scent of burning wood revived my mind. I stood, dusted a few flakes from my pants, and turned.

Eli was toweling himself dry, dressed only in a pair of boxers. For one, two seconds, I stared.

He grinned.

Smug bastard.

"You're still pale." My voice didn't falter. Thank the spirits. "Drop and give me fifty."

He chuckled. "Are you crazy?"

"Fifty pushups." I rolled up the extra towel and snapped it at him.

He hopped to the side to evade its sharp end. "I don't think so."

"Vampire care one-oh-one. If your vampire turns a paler shade of ghostly, make him work out. It works on your brother, and we haven't killed him yet."

"I'm not him." Still, he got on the floor and started on a barrage of pushups. "And since when am I your vampire?"

Ah. Yes. Slip of the tongue, and not at all Freudian in nature. "Figure of speech."

While he entertained me more than he'd ever suspect with the intricate up and down of his muscles, I placed another log on the fire, then got changed into dry clothes myself. As expected, his pants were on the tight side. My drenched, mud-crusted clothes remained on the floor where I'd dropped them. The next time I'd touch them would be with tongs.

"I know where Florian hides the potato chips." I took a longing look at the interplay of his muscles and his tight, well-defined butt. "What do you say?"

"Divine retribution for everything he's ever put us through." He didn't even sound out of breath.

Breathing, of course, was optional for vampires. Oxygen, on the other hand, wasn't. Without it, their brain cells would starve, and they'd get weaker. Within months, they'd be husks of their former selves.

"Yup. I'll go get them." I lingered for a moment, licked my lips, and eventually left to fetch our snack.

By the time I returned, he was dressed. A trace of healthy pink had settled in his cheeks.

"Look at you." His gaze roamed along my body. "Put decent clothes on you, and the anal retentiveness you wear like a badge of honor is gone."

"You do say the sweetest things." I threw the bag of chips at him.

Then we sat on the wooden floor by the fire, silently nursing our beers and our thoughts.

Eli had spread the pages of research and *Hard and Sweet*'s useless financial records out next to him, as if he truly believed they'd help us find Jack.

"At least you achieved one thing tonight." I lifted the can in a half-assed toast. "Vanguard must take you seriously now."

"I don't know." Eli's blank face melted into a solemn expression. "That feels petty now. I guess what I really wanted was to get justice."

"Me too." I drank deep and let the beer oil my throat and soothe my stomach. "I still can't believe Jack set this whole thing up. And Lathan? Does he think he can get away with letting a murderer walk?"

"Honestly, his decision surprises me." Eli's gaze flitted across my face. "The minor kinlords couldn't fight him by themselves, but Mehmet's power has always kept Lathan from crossing the line. He'll take Lathan's actions as an attack on the status quo. If

Mehmet unites with the other kinlords, the demons will be outclassed."

"And yet..."

Eli pulled out his smooth communication stone. "Give me some space, okay?"

"You want space, you move." I waved a limp hand at him. "I don't have the energy."

"To dodge a well-aimed punch?" He expelled a mean chuckle and shooed me away. "Go."

Reluctantly, I followed his pointed finger and crawled out of his stone's field of view.

"You surprise me, Eli." Mehmet's face didn't leave us waiting this time. "Didn't I tell you I'd contact *you*?"

The threat in his voice was enough to give me the chills. Eli had to hate this tight-rope walk between using Mehmet's goodwill and showing deference.

"I'm sorry, sir, but the situation got worse. We found our killer, a demon of no importance, but he had crucial information about Lathan."

"He did?" Mehmet squinted. "Go on."

"Yes, sir. This demon was planning to send poisoned candy bars to Alethia. Once we'd caught him, Lathan ordered Vanguard to release him. That's as much proof as we need to be sure that Lathan is the puppet master."

"This time, you're wrong." Mehmet shook his head. "My sources discovered the illegal shipment coming through the IEA's gate was intended for the satyrs. Can you believe it? But don't worry, I have already taken them into custody."

"The satyrs? But if that's true, why would Lathan arrange for the killer's release?" Eli shot me a quick glance.

I responded with a shrug, just as confused.

"Oh, Eli, my sweet boy. Would Lathan truly care about one man's life? I fear your director may have lied to you. You know he is jealous of your success."

I thought back, trying to recall Vanguard's words. Had I missed another lie?

"You've given me much food for thought, sir." Eli dropped his shoulders. "I thank you."

"Of course. But don't make a habit of calling me for all your cases, or I'm beginning to think sponsoring you was a mistake."

"No, sir. I won't."

Mehmet graciously nodded, and then his face vanished.

"The satyrs are working with Jack?" I shifted back to my previous position next to Eli. "That makes no sense."

"Jack's been working with a sandman. Maybe he's teamed up with a few satyrs, too. Then again..." Eli skimmed a couple of pages. "Here. I thought so. One of the kids that died was a satyr. Why would they collaborate with a demon to kill one of their own?"

"Two demons. Don't forget Vanguard."

"Actually, I'm not convinced yet that he's involved. He let Jack go, but I can come up with two reasons why he would have just like that." He snapped his fingers.

"And they are?"

"First, just because. Never forget the director's one annoying, giant ass." He winced. "Second, Jack's his informant. That earns you a lot of latitude."

"Even for murder? That's cold. Maybe we should ask Jack when we find him." I scratched my waist where my pants were digging in. "He might be hiding out with the satyrs. In that case, he might still be in town."

"Or with fellow demons, although I'm told they're less welcoming." Eli swigged his beer before straightening. "I wish we could ask Vanguard. I have many, many questions."

Eli might doubt the arrogant director's guilt, but interrogating him would still satisfy an itch of mine. "How untouchable is he?"

"If we can get Lathan to disavow him, he's toast." Eli's taut figure swiveled toward me so that he no longer had to twist his neck. "That would mean cooperating with the demon kinlord, though. He'd want to know details of our investigation. Maybe use it as an excuse to destroy the satyrs in Alethia."

"That could create a power imbalance." I kicked out my leg. Hadn't our efforts earned us even one lousy break? "Besides, Ivy and Parker would kill me if I worked with him."

"Yes, but they have no say over me. If you went home and pretended to not know—"

"No way." I raised a hand, putting an end to his nonsense. "First of all, lies among werewolves always come out. Secondly, we've already decided to see this through together."

For a few minutes, we sat and sipped our beers in silence. I examined every move we made, every step we took, in search of new leads or unexplored threads.

"Why go after kids and teenagers?" I asked. "When we thought Lathan was responsible, I was like, sure, that makes sense. He's evil. But on the whole, satyrs don't seem deranged. Ivy's part satyr, and she's pretty normal, considering."

"I can only speculate." Eli lifted his can to his mouth again and took another deep swig. "If the satyr kinlord truly wanted to strengthen his position in Alethia, he could do worse than weaken the other kin. Take out their kids, spread chaos. If handled right, something like this could elevate his status and might."

Once again Eli's ruthless mind had conjured up an answer I could barely believe. The satyrs I knew, here in my world, seemed like good people, but Alethia was a cesspool of manias and power struggles. Maybe life in the kin realm was bad enough to corrupt even a satyr's good judgement.

Eli slapped a hand against his thigh. "I'm an idiot. Remember the shipment of candy bars to the portal?"

"You don't think Jack's still going ahead?"

"I think he'll do exactly that." Eli leaned to his side and thumbed through the pages of evidence. "He doesn't know we know what we know. He thinks Vanguard has stopped the investigation."

Alethia housed the worst of the worst and shouldn't be my concern, but it was also home to thousands upon thousands of innocent kin. We couldn't allow Jack's plan to succeed.

"Still, there's nothing we can do about it. Not as long as Vanguard's the director. Lathan might not help us even if we asked." Eli set down his beer and brushed his hand over his hair. "And we can't involve your pack. Are we fucked?"

"Possibly." I gave a toothy, red-carpet smile. "And not in a good way."

Eli bumped my shoulder with his. "Now you're stealing my lines."

"Sorry."

"Don't apologize." He bent his legs at the knees and stared at me openly. "Just wondering if your jokes are backed by intent or merely empty flirting?"

Hell, I couldn't answer that. Not only did my tongue suddenly take a time-out, my brain calculated the consequences of both potential replies at light speed, to no avail. I didn't do one-night stands, but Eli wasn't like other guys. Other guys didn't leave me lost for words. Maybe, this once, I could stop my hunt for Mr. Perfect, even if his first name was 'Right-Now.'

A trace of daring lightness crept over Eli's expression. "In that case…"

He tilted forward, his eyes bright blue and clear, his mouth perfectly shaped. I didn't breathe, wasn't sure if I even could. He took the can from my hand and deposited it next to me. My gaze was locked on his face, his dimple, his lips.

A phone rang. Not mine.

Eli stilled.

No fucking way. My body was primed for a mind-spinning kiss, my tongue ready to taste him.

The phone's generic ringtone got louder.

"So close," he mumbled and turned around to pick up his cell. "Hey, Min— ... Are you sure? ... No, stay. Don't tell anyone. Okay?"

He slowly disconnected the call and massaged his forehead.

"What's wrong?" I asked.

"It's Jack."

"Of course it is." I blew out the breath I'd been holding before remembering what he'd done. "You have a lead?"

"Now, don't blow your stack."

"Okay." I eyed him cautiously. "When have you ever seen me be anything but calm?"

"Right." His brief chuckle stopped abruptly. "Jack... Well, he got himself killed."

CHAPTER FOURTEEN

"Jack's really dead?" I breathed hard, even though sitting in the passenger seat of my car didn't exactly tax my lungs. "How? When?"

"Mina was on her way back to the office and came across a familiar smell." Eli sounded as incredulous as I felt. "She's a kitsune, a fox shapeshifter, and her sense of smell is—"

"Highly accurate."

"Perfect for sniffing out blood." Eli's driving almost approached speed limit. "Jack's been got bad, she says, less than a mile from the office."

"So close?" I jerked my head toward him. "How did anyone even know he was there?"

"No idea. Hey, do you werewolves have a clean-up crew? Normally I'd get our guys to do it, but I don't want Vanguard to know about Jack's death."

"A clean-up crew? No." I retrieved my phone. "But I've got a guy."

"Not Florian." Once again, he just about spat out his brother's name.

"Calm down. It's not Florian."

Despite the early hours, I didn't have to wait long for Rollo to answer the phone.

"Ali? 's that you?" His deep voice rumbled from the other end of the line. "You know what time it is, dude?"

"I need you to wake up and listen. Get dressed, sneak out without anyone seeing you, and come meet me at..." I looked at Eli.

"Cannon Park, east exit," he said.

"Meet me at Cannon Park, east exit. Oh, and bring plenty of plastic sheeting."

"Why?" Rollo laughed. "Did you kill anyone?"

This would be the last time he'd laugh in a while. "Just make it quick."

He didn't quibble. I was Rollo's superior. He accepted any order that came his way with a smile, even if it meant breaking the rules now and again.

Heidi's death would test his positivity.

I disconnected the call and pushed my phone into my pocket.

Despite Jack's assurances of being a great crime boss, someone had taken the fight to him. Had the satyrs received orders to take him out?

Not ten minutes later, Eli parked the car on a largely empty street. Stars flickered behind the haze of black cloud that spanned across the sky, and the moon lit the way into the park. Mina and Jack were situated not far from the main path. The medical examiner held a tray of drinks in one hand and a folded-down umbrella in the other. Her lab coat had been replaced by a jacket that barely reached her waist.

Eli hadn't exaggerated. Jack had been got good. I let the sight and smell of blood that surrounded the body wash over me. The wet ground had drained away much of it, but the spectacle remained gruesome. As expected, not a pang of guilt or conscience shifted inside me. My wolf, for one, was giving a satisfied moan.

Eli bent over, taking shallow breaths.

"You okay?" I stepped forward, placing my body between him and Jack's blood.

"Yeah." He straightened and retreated a few inches. "But I will have to feed soon."

The bushes and trees were denser on this side of the park than in the west where grass areas invited kids to play soccer and run around.

"Over there." Mina had spotted a blond woman jogging in the dark.

"Might as well steer her away from the scene while you're at it." I gave Eli an encouraging nod. "We don't want her getting the shock of her life."

All three of us knew the jogger wasn't headed our way, and, frankly, her emotional stability wasn't as much of a concern as preventing Eli from faltering.

"I—" Eli's mouth turned down as he lowered his gaze. "I'll be right back."

He sped off and caught up with the jogger within a few seconds. The woman slowed and aimed a warm smile at him, wrapped up in his glamour.

That left me with the dead body and a kitsune. Mina didn't give the appearance of someone concerned by anything—not by my presence, and least of all not by the dead guy at her feet. She seemed content waiting, like me, for Eli's return.

He led his meal behind a tree farther up the path, where benches and lampposts lined the grass edges. They slid effortlessly into the dark where no one would watch him sate himself. Afterward, he'd fill her mind with beautiful memories to replace the ones of their encounter. How would it feel to be held by Eli, to let his teeth sink into my skin? I half-closed my eyes and wrapped the thought around me.

"He's shy about feeding in front of people," Mina said before slurping from the straw of one of her three drinks.

"Weird because Eli's not shy in any other respect." I rolled my hands into fists since I couldn't think of what else to do with them. "Not at all."

"He's got his eccentricities, for sure." She giggled.

Yeah, death didn't bother her.

The park looked different tonight. As if the trees I knew had gone home and been replaced by more ominous versions of themselves. Change had flooded the world between the hours of midnight and dawn. Yesterday, I'd been an accountant who accepted the company of numbers over that of people. Now, without taking to arms or marching into combat, I'd become a warrior. A pursuer of truth who found justice in the empty eyes of the man responsible for Heidi's death. Of course, his body couldn't give life back to my girl. His loss would not be her gain, nor would his lost energy spark her smile or trigger her laughter. But Jack's demise brought me a step closer to closure.

What next? Would Lathan and Mehmet wipe out the satyrs, ringing in a new era of the *six* kinlords? And if satyrs became enemies, would Ivy be safe? As for me, my priority would be to see the end of Vanguard's directorship. He bore at least some responsibility for Heidi's death. Maybe he'd even been complicit.

"Milkshake?" Mina held out the cardboard tray. "I insist."

As bizarre as the situation was, a sugar hit was just what the doctor ordered.

"Thanks. Any mystery to *his* death?" I pointed my chin at Jack's body, lit poorly by artificial diffused light.

"None." Mina gestured with the pointy end of her umbrella. "Stabs, cuts, slashes. Best guess, one attacker. Strong. Right-handed. And definitely pissed."

"Yeah." I crouched and surreptitiously considered my environment while sucking cold shake through my paper straw.

Was the killer still around? Or had he gone home to send his kids off to school?

"I'm not sad but definitely disappointed he's dead." Eli suddenly stood next to me, the third shake in his hand. "I just really wish you could have delivered him to Parker."

I hadn't even heard his footsteps. Yup, Eli was back to his stealthy vampire self. His face had lost its paleness, no push-ups required. He joined me in a crouch to check Jack's pockets.

"Empty except for his phone." He rose again and looked at the medical examiner. "How long ago?"

"Not long," Mina said. "Maybe an hour, no more than three. I'll know more once I get him on the table."

"This must be Vanguard's doing." I shot to my feet. "No one else knew he was even here. I mean, it's not a random killing, is it?"

"With at least ten victims to Jack's name, actually there's no shortage of suspects." Eli shook his head at Mina to stop her from asking questions. "Vanguard isn't the only one with a motive."

He was right. The kin families who'd lost their kids would

make equally likely culprits. "Are you saying Clarence informed his people about Jack's release?"

Mina could also be related to one of the victims, and she *had* found the body. But it would have been impolite to voice my theories in front of her.

"Hang on there." For the first time, Mina's posture tensed. "Vanguard? I don't even need to hear about this motive to know he's mentally and physically capable of this. But Clarence? No way."

"Sorry." I offered a conciliatory smile. "I don't think he had anything to do with it either."

"It had to have been personal, though." Eli dragged his words as he tapped on the touch display of Jack's cell. "A random robbery would be too much of a coincidence. I'm checking his call log."

As always, Eli didn't simply speculate but turned his musings into action. I should have thought of that. Normally, my brain worked faster than this.

"Jack made a five-minute call to an unknown number." Eli got out his own phone and made a call. "Hey, Clarence. One more favor. Can you trace this number for me?" He read out the digits, then waited. "Really? Interesting. Thanks, buddy."

I raised my eyebrows.

"Remember the shipment that's scheduled for this morning?" He tapped his nose with his phone. "Jack's last call was to the delivery company."

"Whoa." Rollo approached from behind the bushes. "That dude's all kinds of dead."

He'd been smart enough to dress up in bad-weather gear.

"You must be Rollo." Eli lifted a hand. "Heard much about you. Only good things."

All six foot three of Rollo beamed. "Florian talks about you all the time as well."

"Right." Eli shot me a loaded look. He hadn't missed the fact that Florian, apparently, didn't have good things to say about him. "That lovely lady there's Mina."

"Hi there." Rollo shook Mina's elbow since she didn't have a hand free.

"Listen, kid." I coughed. "Last night, I found a body on our doorstep."

"What?" He stared at Jack. "Not cool."

"Not him." Oh shit. "It was Heidi."

"Heidi who?" His eyes flashed from me to Eli, then to Mina, and back to me. Then he took two steps back. "No. Why would you even say that? Not our Heidi. She's asleep. At home." He half-turned away, forlorn. "I know she is."

Eli nudged me and jerked his head toward the young wolf. He didn't get that, as Rollo's superior, I typically gave orders, not hugs. An unexpected show of feelings, even to comfort him, might wig the kid out completely.

"I don't get it." Rollo's large eyes brought back the lump in my throat I'd done well to suppress. "Why would she be dead?"

Eli pushed me, less subtly this time, toward Rollo.

"Come here." I gathered the tall wolf close in that forced way women made fun of.

He didn't stiffen, only buried his head in my neck. His hands hung loosely by his side at first and eventually moved up to cling to me.

"I'm sorry. I really am." I tightened my embrace, selfishly soaking up his presence. After feeling cold all night, his touch infused me with warmth.

He was younger than me, closer to Heidi's age, and although his size sometimes let me forget it, his compassion often got the better of him. Right now, he needed kindness, even if it was me offering it. Or maybe, especially because it was me.

Our alpha didn't just dish out growls but plenty of attaboys, too. An appreciative nod from him could swell anyone's chest. A kind word could calm any soul, no matter how troubled.

Maybe this is what my embrace meant to Rollo. A promise that things would be okay—because he wasn't alone.

"What happened?" He lifted his head, his eyes brimming with tears, and quickly wiped them. "Was it an accident?"

"This guy…" I jerked my head at Jack's body. "He's the one who killed her."

"Did you do that to him?" Rollo turned to examine Jack's wounds. "Fucking hell, dude."

"Sadly, it wasn't me." I prodded him upright and held his gaze. "You're going to have to keep it together right now, okay?"

He nodded.

"When you get home, tell Parker. Only him." I squeezed Rollo's shoulder to get him to focus. "Tell him the killer's dead. I'll be back later and will explain everything. Okay?"

"Wait. You're not coming home?" Rollo's voice turned icy. "Man, Parker's gonna be pissed."

"He'll be fine." He was right, though. Making him do my dirty work wasn't fair.

Parker deserved to hear about Heidi from me.

"Excuse us." Eli dragged me aside, out of earshot. "Maybe you should go home, Ali. We've done enough, haven't we?"

"I think we can be reasonably certain that Vanguard killed Jack." I jerked my gaze back to where the demon's body sprawled. "After all, Jack has served his purpose. And if they were partners, I want the director punished, too."

"You have no proof he was even involved." Yet Eli didn't sound as if he disagreed. "We only know he let Jack go."

"You want proof?" I skimmed my gaze across the trees and, behind them, to the gradually brightening sky. "When Vanguard told us the investigation was over, he had a wet patch on his shirt, and his shoes were wet, too. That's because he'd been out here with Jack, killing him."

"I nearly slipped in the hallway." Eli squinted. "But that's hardly evidence one way or the other."

"The candy bars will be picked up at seven. If Vanguard worked with Jack, he might oversee the shipment himself." I gestured toward the road. "Let's go and see for ourselves. If we can stop the candy bars from getting into Alethia, shouldn't we do so?"

Eli's frown intensified. "I doubled the guard. They'll handle whatever comes their way."

"Except Vanguard is their boss. For all we know, they're helping him." I slapped my hand into the palm of the other to add urgency to my plan. "I'd call backup, but Parker must weigh all the pros and cons of any action he undertakes. We can't wait that long."

"I don't know." Shifting on his feet, Eli turned his head away. "Mehmet took the satyrs into custody. I'll contact him, and he'll make sure the candy bars won't cause harm if they do make it across."

"Come on, man. Think. Mehmet's no more trustworthy than Jack, Vanguard, or indeed Lathan." I grabbed his arm and forced him to stand still. "Why are you suddenly so cautious? You of all people should be dying to bust Vanguard's ass."

"Trust me. I'd love to give the director a good beating, but he's my boss. This—working for the IEA—is my job."

"So what?"

"If they find out I'm the one who told *you*—not just an outsider, but a werewolf—of our portal, my career is over."

"Even if you're right and you save thousands of people in the process?"

"Even then." Eli steered his gaze past me and then onto the ground. "Who's going to believe us anyway? We don't have one solid piece of evidence against him. It'll be Vanguard's word against mine."

Was my hunch worth Eli's job?

Jack was dead, and Heidi was avenged. What did I, a werewolf, care about the people of Alethia anyway? Besides, I couldn't say for sure if Vanguard had a hand in any of the killings, or if he was merely a stakeholder in Jack's candy bar scheme—or maybe not even that.

Eli fixated me with a focused look. "I need this job. Without it, what will I do? Besides, I'm good at it, for fuck's sake."

"Yes, you are." I took a few steps to the side and then back, running my hand through my hair while my mind worked feverishly on a solution. "Okay, how about this. You have your phone, right? We could film the director in action. We don't even have to engage if it's too dangerous."

He shook his head but then stilled. Bit his lip. Raised and lowered his eyebrows as if having and dismissing ideas too quickly to put into words. Eventually, he crossed his arms, clearly not yet ready to make a decision that could change his life.

"The other kinlords will recognize your efforts and could even make you the director." I leaned in and lowered my voice. "Your grand-sire will help smooth things over. You'll get everything you ever wanted."

"Mehmet likes my groveling ass, but probably not that much. I don't think you get how big of a deal telling you about the portal is. Even if we prove Vanguard's behind it all, I'll still get kicked out of Silverton."

I slumped my shoulders, fresh all out of arguments. Did the other kin hate us werewolves that much? Maybe it was their love of secrecy and intrigue that would drive them to punish Eli for doing the right thing.

Pushing Eli into going to the portal despite his reservations would make me no better than them. He didn't deserve to be torn apart by different loyalties. As for Vanguard... If he was dirty, he'd slip up again. Parker would make sure to keep his eye on him.

"Fine. You win. No portal." I sent Eli an understanding smile. "Although it's a shame. I was looking forward to going rogue with you."

"Yeah?" Eli's blue eyes were painfully wide. "If you put it that way, I might change my mind."

"No. Jack's dead. That will be enough for today." I leaned my head to the side. "Remember, partners always have each other's backs."

"Okay. Thanks. I... I appreciate that." He made to head back to Mina but stopped before he'd taken his first step.

"What's wrong?" I asked.

Inch by inch, he turned toward me again. "You're right. Partners do have each other's backs."

"Yeah." I chuckled. "That's what I just said."

His expression was devoid of fun or pain. "You've had my back all night. Maybe it's time I returned the favor."

"Not if the stakes are that high." I waved him off. "It's not worth it."

"If we don't find evidence, I'll have to continue working for Vanguard. That might actually be worse than going on the run."

"You've managed so far."

"That was when I thought he was just a spiteful, jealous jerk." Eli spread his arms in a resigned shrug. "Now I know he's worse. He allowed a murderer to walk. How can I pursue justice if my boss treats it like a solution in a crossword puzzle?"

I barely moved, afraid he might change his mind again. "You really want to risk it?"

"As you said. We'll use our phones to get footage. Maybe we'll catch Vanguard carrying boxes or giving orders. And if you stay quiet, no one will even know you were there."

That might work. Once we had proof, Eli could convince the IEA to disavow the director. And then, he'd be fair game for my pack.

Our gazes locked for a few seconds, and I smiled. "If you're sure."

"Absolutely." Eli resumed walking, raising a hand to beckon me along. "Come on then."

As usual, he'd made up his mind, and all I could do was keep up. It wasn't so much that he was a control freak. No, his drive came from an innate sense of fairness. As fond as he was of all the shades of gray the world had to offer, he still knew black from white —and right from wrong.

I paced after him, doing all I could to hide my grin. "You surprise me all the time."

"I surprise me, too. But we'd better be right about this." He kicked a small branch on the ground, which tumbled into the bushes. "Fuck. Of all the times to show a rebellious streak, this is the moment you pick."

"What can I say? Your daredevil attitude is infectious."

Back at the crime scene, Rollo looked lost in thought, not paying attention to Mina, who kept the conversation going by herself.

I mouthed a 'thank you' in her direction.

"Okay. Let's get organized." Eli clapped once loud enough to make Rollo flinch. "Do you have a place to do an autopsy on Jack's body?"

"You want me to do an autopsy?" Rollo pinched his hand to his chest.

"You could give it a go—young, enterprising man that you are— but I was thinking this once, Mina might perform it for you." Eli smiled at the medical examiner. "I gotta warn you. Vanguard officially closed the case. Things are going to get ugly at the office soon if we have our way."

"I'll do this autopsy not for work, but for fun. Let's call it a hobby." She tittered. "Sue me."

"Thank you." He brushed his hand over her cheek for a second before turning his attention back to Rollo. "You only need to provide the space. Once Mina's done with it, the body's Parker's."

"Okay. Sure." Rollo's eyes were still glazed. "What about Heidi?"

"She's in the Volvo." My words hurt almost on a physical level. Heidi lay dead in my trunk. How graceless. How mundane. How cruel the world was.

"I'll transfer her to your car and get the sheeting." Eli took the keys from the kid's hand. "You did bring it, right?"

"Huh?" Rollo's expression rolled shut. "I did, yes. Mine's the truck behind Ali's Volvo."

That was it. Rollo was back in the game and motivated to do his job. Compartmentalizing was a virtue in our pack.

Eli had already shot off through the iron gates of the park.

A breeze caressed my neck, where not too long ago, my long hair had provided shelter against the elements. Having it cut short had marked a departure for me, a step outside my routine. How ridiculous to have attached this much meaning to a minor change. Consistency was good, but occasionally, flexibility was better. Rollo, despite being younger than me, had known this instinctively. Being yanked out of his sleep to take care of a body probably didn't even rate as unusual to him.

Heidi's death was a different matter, of course.

For a while, a thick silence stretched between us. The kid would get his answers soon enough, but not until I had the full picture myself.

"You off to a bar then?" Rollo asked.

"Of course not."

"Why aren't you coming home then? Parker needs to know."

"You're going to tell him." I narrowed my eyes. Why did he keep arguing?

"Why me?" he asked.

"Because if I called him, he'd order me to come back." I lowered my voice. I can't do that yet."

"That's the part I don't get." Rollo used his height to intimidate me. "I've never seen you chicken out of anything."

"Pipe down, kid." If I had Parker's powers, I could magically instill calm. Since I didn't, I had to use my voice to discipline him. My broad shoulders for once came in handy. "That's an order."

Rollo growled.

That kid had balls, I gave him that. I growled back, louder, and bared my teeth, until he stopped and dropped his head.

"Here." Eli returned and forcefully stuffed the plastic tarp into Rollo's hand. The muscles under his eyes twitched. "Go easy on Ali, man. He and I have been out here for hours, running down not one, but two murderers, so give him some fucking space, will ya?"

Rollo leaned back. Despite his height and impressive build, he knew that pissing off a vampire was even less smart than challenging me.

And Eli had sounded damn scary.

"Let's all take a step back." I gripped Eli's shoulder to nudge him away from Rollo. "I promise I'll fill you in later, kid, but I need to finish this before I talk to Parker."

"No, I get it." Rollo rubbed a spot on his forehead. "I mean... Sorry, man. I'm just..."

"Me too."

We exchanged a glance that required no more words on the matter.

"Mina's gonna drive your pickup." Eli handed her Rollo's key without taking his eyes off the kid, but at least he'd taken the bite out of his voice. "You do the heavy lifting, not the delicate driving maneuvers. I've seen what stress has done to Ali's steering, and it's not pretty. Less road kill, more road *skill* is our motto today."

"I can do that." Rollo took his orders like a pro.

Despite his age, he'd seen a lot of crap in his life. He'd earned his place as our top enforcer because he was tough and knew when to knuckle down.

"Okay then. We're off." Eli threw the keys to my car in my direction. "Try not to kill us."

CHAPTER FIFTEEN

We climbed into the Volvo, and I set off toward Lawton's Bridge, an almost derelict structure outside of town. Traffic was heavier now than it had been all night, and while the alcohol in my system didn't affect me, lack of sleep certainly did.

"By the way. What's wrong with the way I drive?" I squinted at Eli.

"I'll let you know when it happens. All I can say for sure is that you fly way too low." Once again, he'd gripped the door handle, even though I barely touched the accelerator. "I'm just surprised your usual caution doesn't extend to the road."

I braked hard, and the sudden deceleration yanked his torso forward.

"Better?" I grinned.

"Forget I said anything."

"Gladly." I flattened the gas pedal. "Besides, you were the one who insisted we take my car."

The clock was approaching seven o'clock, the time the shipment was scheduled—and also the hour Parker typically got up. My demotion was all but guaranteed, but if I could prove Vanguard's complicity *and* provide Jack's dead body, I might convince Parker to not kick me out. I didn't have anywhere to go. Returning to my parents wasn't an option, and living as a rogue wouldn't do much for my life expectancy.

To save my ass, Eli and I would first need to catch the director in the act. At least, my partner had grace and stealth on his side. My only chance of success was getting there early. Finding an advantageous location before Vanguard arrived would mean I wouldn't have to sneak up to him.

As I rounded the corner onto another road, my tires lost traction. The car's rear broke away, steering us toward the sidewalk.

"Damn." I quickly regained control. "Sorry."

Eli whimpered.

"Out of curiosity, what would you do if you did become the new director?" I kept my hands rolled tight around the steering wheel so as not to give Eli more ammunition in his campaign against my driving skills.

"Improve our relationship with all races of kin." Eli crawled out of his metaphorical turtle shell and straightened in his seat, although his pathological attachment to the safety handle remained.

"Interesting. Why would that be your priority?"

"I don't know about these ominous warnings about Lathan breaking out of Alethia or about the imminent apocalypse we've been hearing, but it's time we weaned ourselves off our dependence on the kinlords. We need our own community, where everyone plays a part."

"Do you even think that's possible?" I took the next bend slower than I had the last one. "Aren't the prejudices too ingrained?"

"I don't think we can eliminate them tomorrow, no, but we have to start. Because one day, something terrible *will* happen. Lathan or Mehmet could return, or the humans discover our existence and begin wiping us out. Either way, we must close the gap between the races now, not when we're in trouble."

Eli was a dreamer. Who knew? But then, maybe his idealism had been there all night.

"If anyone can perform that miracle, you can." I smiled more for myself than for him. "You invited me—a werewolf—into the IEA. Better yet, you combined the skills of a troll, a kitsune, a werewolf, and a vampire to solve a heinous crime. It will take the kin community months to recover from Jack's actions, but if they knew of the cooperation you made possible, it might make dealing with the aftermath easier. Because they'd know they're no longer alone."

"Oh boy." Eli chuckled.

"What's so funny?" I leaned forward to read the sign at the side of the road. Only a couple of minutes to our destination.

"All of it." He released the handle and dropped his hand onto his leg. "Hearing my plan spoken out loud, it sounds naïve."

"Not naïve, Eli. Hopeful. There's nothing wrong with that."

At last, we'd reached the unpaved road to Lawton's Bridge. Across the flat landscape and distant woods, the new day finally dawned. For once, it would bring not a new beginning but rather an end. My life would never be the same, whatever fate had in store.

A particularly deep hole ripped the steering wheel out of my hands, but my reflexes saved me from an embarrassing detour into a field.

"See that old barn?" Eli pointed his finger, his body still relaxed. "The portal's inside."

The barn was the only building out here, not counting the burned-out ruins of a farmhouse about fifty yards away.

I rolled the Volvo onto the grass behind a grouping of bushes and turned off the engine.

"No one's here yet." I tapped the clock on my dashboard. "Ten minutes early. We should get into position."

"Parking's round the back, which means Vanguard could

already be here. Hang on." Eli dialed a number on his cell and pressed the device against his right ear. "Clarence. Me again. I assume the director's no longer at the office? ... That's what I thought. Any idea when he left? ... Thanks. ... No, that's all. I'll call you later."

He disconnected and let the phone sink into his lap. "Vanguard's no longer at the office."

"Buck up, fang boy." I gripped the door handle. "If we get the proof we need, he'll be done ordering you around."

We got out of the car, armed ourselves with our phones at the ready, and approached the gray wooden building with our senses on alert. The air was still and yet felt heavy, although whether from past rain or my nerves I couldn't say. Without bushes or trees to conceal our approach, we relied on silence. Eli's light, elegant gait made easy work of it, but my size was more of a hinderance. I kept my gaze glued to the ground, ensuring I didn't splash the puddles or slip in the mud.

We slid along the barn wall toward the rear. Eli lifted his free hand and stopped. The sound of voices reached my ears. I nodded at him to indicate I was aware, and he peeked his head around the corner.

Without a direct line of sight, I relied on my senses to catch movement on the wet ground. Two sets of feet walking—no, trudging and slipping—through the mud into the building. My gut grew tight like a coiled spring. How outmanned were we? What would Vanguard do if he spotted us?

A few seconds later, Eli beckoned me to retreat a few feet.

"I didn't see the director." His whispered words sounded shallow. "Only a delivery truck. They're unpacking now."

"What's the plan?" I, too, kept my voice low. "Should we film them?"

"If Vanguard's not here, we could try and take them out. See if they have papers that trace back to him."

"I'm all for playing the hero, but none of the documents we've found so far even hinted at Vanguard's participation." I shook my phone in the air to underline my words. "If we want to catch him out, I say we find a hiding spot and wait for him to arrive."

That was, assuming my suspicions were right. Had I got this wrong from the start? I'd found no evidence that Vanguard was part of Jack's organization. As Eli had pointed out earlier, Jack had been the IEA's informant. Maybe Vanguard had struck a deal with him—Jack's life in exchange for dirt on an even worse crime boss.

"Okay, but not out here." Eli gestured toward the barn's entrance. "We should slip inside."

"Wonderful," I muttered. "Do you have a plan B in case they see us or the director pops in later?"

"Of course I have a plan B." Eli's jaw muscles seemed ultra-tight. "If we're spotted, we dazzle them with fang and fur, and hope Vanguard's level of power is more a toddler's than Godzilla."

"I know coming here was my idea, but it's not what I'd call a solid plan."

"No, it does lack a certain finesse."

"Maybe I should call in the pack after all."

"Now he tells me."

I sighed. "Running into danger all Rambo-style seemed more romantic in my head."

"If it's any consolation, if you die, you'll still be my hero." He gave me a thumbs-up.

"Who says I'm going to die?"

"First of all, the black guy always bites the dust first." His impish grin—and that irresistible dimple—were back. "Second of all, I'm the fucking assistant director of the IEA. No way am *I* gonna die."

"Your comforting words have given me a real boost, you know?" I laughed nervously.

"Nothing's going to happen to you." He placed his hand behind my neck and squeezed lightly. "I won't allow it."

Yeah, because that's the way the world worked.

Still, the calm in his eyes filled me with confidence. Or rather, with the vague hope that I'd live to receive my deserved reprimand from Parker in due time.

Eli slid back to the barn's corner, held up his hand to keep me from breaking cover too early, then moved into the open.

The semi-truck towed a trailer, which stood with its back wide open. The cargo hold was only about half full, although I had no idea how many parcels had been inside originally. As a rough estimate, it could have contained as many as fifteen-hundred boxes, each with hundreds of candy bars. That many candy bars could do serious damage to the stability of Alethia—and kill too many kids.

The barn's door stood open at an angle. If I'd stumbled across this place on a walk, no way would I have mistaken it for the home of the IEA's secret portal to Alethia.

Voices approached from inside, and we built ourselves up on either side of the entrance.

"... can't believe Tiana got the drop on him," a woman said. "Couldn't have happened to a nicer fella, though."

She strode out first, all six feet of her, followed a step behind by a shorter guy. Ordinary kin like me couldn't distinguish trolls from humans, but something told me these delivery people were demons.

Were they aware that, by following Jack's orders, they weren't doing Lathan's bidding but the satyrs'?

"Shouldn't he be here by now?" The man checked his watch. "He's late."

Thankfully, their ears couldn't pick up my accelerated heartbeat.

"I'll check." He turned abruptly—and saw me. His eyes widened. "Who are you?"

Eli grabbed the woman and took her out with a slice to her throat. A second later, I brought my fist to bear down on the guy, who barely had time to register my movement before he joined his female companion in the mud. I didn't check whether either was still alive, because honestly? I didn't want to know.

"Slight wrinkle to plan A." Eli dragged their bodies around the corner, away from prying eyes, then he approached the entrance to peek inside.

"I'm not yet ready for plan B, though." I stared at his shoulder, waiting for his verdict.

"Eight people packing crates, plus six guards on the ground, probably unconscious." He frowned. "If I hadn't doubled their number—"

"This is Jack's fault, not yours," I said. "Besides, you had to at least try to keep the portal secure."

"Maybe. Anyway, keep your eyes peeled. Vanguard might be in there."

We slipped inside the barn, which smelled of rotting wood and corroded metal. Old agricultural equipment stood near the entrance, from an old tractor to a rusty wheelbarrow and a trailer that was past its expiration date. The walls at the back of the barn, typically dark enough to block both sound and light from the outside, were bathed in the glow from a shimmering, rippling puddle hovering about a foot above the ground —the portal. The white noise coming from its center rivaled that of the Madakaripura Waterfall my parents and I visited when I was a kid.

Six men loaded boxes labeled *Hard and Sweet* into a container, presumably one fortified with magic to survive the trip to Alethia. Their conversation was muted, partly blocked by the whooshing noise from the portal itself.

But it was another bright source of light that drew my attention. The holographic face of a man with long, blond hair—lighter even than Eli's—hovered high above the workers and tracked their progress. His cruel Elvis-type twist lifted his upper lip.

Fuck me. I'd just got my first glimpse of Lathan. He looked every bit as Ivy had described. But why was he here, overseeing the shipment, instead of the satyrs? He'd never stoop to working with the weaker races.

The hologram of another man's face flickered, a little fainter, to Lathan's left.

"Is that who I think it is?" I whispered, forcing the air from my lung.

Holding his phone up to film the scene, Eli crouched behind a ladder, his teeth bared. "Mehmet."

I studied the vampire kinlord's face more closely, looking for a physical similarity with Eli, even though the two weren't related by blood. Had he warned Lathan about the satyrs' grab for power?

"What's he doing?" I glanced at Eli. "Is he here to catch Vanguard in the act? Like us?"

"Oh, I doubt it." Eli stared at the vampire kinlord with eyes so wide the whites showed clearly even in the dim light.

By the spirits, I was too stupid to live. "The satyrs have never been involved in this scheme, have they? Your grand-sire made the whole thing up. It's been him and Lathan all along."

Mehmet could have served lie after lie to Eli, and I wouldn't have been able to smell his duplicity via his projection.

"Let's find out." Eli motioned for me to seek out a corner closer to the action.

I squatted in a dark spot by an old fridge.

"Hang on." Eli held up his hand. "They're wondering why the boxes have stopped coming."

A vampire's hearing beat mine by miles. Yet judging by the workers' head-scratching, I didn't doubt his assessment.

"What do you want to do?" I asked. "Maybe you should hang back. If Mehmet finds out you're here—"

"Then that's the way it goes." Eli's jaw tensed. "I'm no one's puppet, and definitely not of someone who cooperates with Lathan."

"And your job?"

"The IEA's intertwined with the kinlords. As long as Mehmet

was on my side, there was hope I could change the organization from within."

"You don't think you still can?"

"Not a chance. I always suspected my grand-sire had his own plans, but I never expected this." He clicked the camera feature's stop button and slid his cell into his pack pocket. "Best we can do is stop the poison from getting into Alethia."

"Eight against two." I hardened my voice. "We can do this. Unless these are demon MMA fighters with superpowers, I may not even need to shift."

"Let's pick up a couple of boxes." Eli pointed with two fingers toward the entrance. "The darkness will fool the workers long enough to keep their defenses down until we get close enough."

We slipped out undetected and picked up two boxes each. Even though Eli's speed and easy movements meant he'd be able to invade our opponents' personal space before they even knew it, I was the weak link. Yet he didn't make me feel 'less than.' Rather, he adapted to ensure both of us could play to our strengths.

And I wasn't going to disappoint him.

CHAPTER SIXTEEN

We carried the boxes inside, past the trailer and the wheelbarrow, keeping to the shadows for as long as we could. Lathan's and Mehmet's faces continued to loom like gods over us, and their watchful eyes made my stomach twist. The portal cast a bright circle of light around the crates that were being readied for shipment—too bright to keep our deception concealed for long.

"Finally." One of the eight goons approached us. "We thought Jack's no-show syndrome was catching."

"Hang on, Mike," another man cut through our approach. "That's not Liz."

Eli threw his box at Mike and kicked the other guy in the stomach. His fangs had popped out as easily as knives from their sheaths.

Mike quickly got back upright and pulled Eli toward him, where the portal's glow lit his symmetric features and the lighter shades of his hair. Falling through would be fatal.

"Eli?" Mehmet asked. "What the hell are you doing?"

His tone spoke of betrayal, even though Eli was the one who'd been lied to. Yet the vampire kinlord's reaction only highlighted that the consequences of our actions for Eli's future were immeasurable. This wasn't just about his job anymore—by convincing him to check the portal, I'd catapulted him into mortal danger.

A breeze brushed across my cheek, giving me enough warning to duck the fist that followed it.

I struck my attacker with a double jab but took a blow to my kidney that pushed the air from my lungs. Another strike knocked me off my feet, and I fell. The kinlords' curses alternated with orders to their lieutenants to maim us, torture us, kill us. I wiped across my eyes so I could see again. Why the hell was I always the one that got to eat dirt?

Eli's opponent dropped by my side. His head smacked the floor unprotected, but he wouldn't have felt any pain. He was gone, and his empty eyes looked right through me.

A vibration in the ground warned me of danger, and my wolf didn't need more. I clawed the dust under my palm and rolled swiftly to the side.

The demon called Mike planted his foot where my face had been only a second ago.

I chucked my fistful of grit into his eyes.

He sputtered and coughed, giving me a chance to kick his knees out from under him. He stayed down.

Eli was charging toward the other workers, and I was about to join him when something moved to my left.

"Vanguard." Lathan's voice, not unpleasant by itself, echoed from wall to wall. "Kill the intruders."

Shit. Our odds were beginning to suck.

The director snarled, distorting his face into something scarier than I could have imagined. Maybe he wasn't as incompetent as we'd thought.

My wolf would make short shrift of him, but getting rid of my clothes and shifting into my animal form would take too long. Instead, I struck him, my punch landing just above his nose.

He bowed and covered his face with his hand. "Stop it, you idiot."

Not the reaction I'd been expecting. "Aren't you working with them?"

"Of course not." He glowered past me at Eli. "You told the werewolf about the portal? Are you crazy?"

"Not. The right." Eli landed a title-winning blow to his opponent's right eye socket. "Time."

Mehmet's and Lathan's curses continued, yet stuck in Alethia, they couldn't put their powers to deadly use. Things would be different if the poisoned candy made it through. United, and with the other five races weakened, they might eventually succeed in breaking through to our world.

For now, the remaining workers had abandoned their packing duties to follow the kinlords' orders. Eli and I had already taken two out, and Eli was working on numbers three, four and five.

The last three guys were approaching Vanguard and me. Their squat figures didn't impress me, even in my non-wolf shape—until they pulled knives from their pockets.

"Vanguard." I fixed one of the men with my glare while I circled him. "Did you kill Jack?"

"Of course I did." He, too, moved cautiously in parallel with the other two opponents. "I couldn't just let him go and kill hundreds of children. I'm a father myself."

"You had me fooled." With my attention on my would-be attacker, I couldn't scrutinize the director's expression for the truth. After Jack's success at tricking my lie-detection senses, I no longer trusted my nose alone, although I smelled no deceit.

"I suspected Lathan was up to something. When he ordered me to let Jack go despite the mountain of evidence, the image sharpened."

"You followed him?" I beckoned my adversary with my index finger to encourage his attack.

Vanguard's fancy footwork kept the other guys from charging. "That's when I overheard him give the go-ahead for the shipment, and I came to investigate."

The guy opposite me swished his knife in a crisscross pattern close to his chest, as if trying to fake me out. He wore a mushroom haircut like the Beatles in their heyday, and the seventies clothes to boot.

"Are you actually going to fight me today?" I sighed to signal my boredom.

He pulled his mouth into a smile and swung again.

The moment his blade passed me, I kicked his shin and followed up with a downward punch to his skull. His hand and jaw hung loosely, his eyes lost focus, and I ended his challenge with my knee in his guts and a karate chop to the back of his neck.

He fell onto all fours. A kick to his head took him out.

Vanguard cried out and flailed his arms at one of his attackers, whose blade was covered in dirt. What the hell? Maybe I'd *over*estimated the director.

I leaped at the man and bulldozed him to the ground.

"Fuck!" the guy shouted as we fell.

I landed on top and ground his ugly visage into the powdery dust. For once, it wasn't me licking dirt.

He sputtered and coughed, his closed eyes robbing him of the chance to see my thump coming. I barely tapped his ear, and his movements stopped.

"That's my brother." One of Eli's opponents, shorter than the guy I'd just felled, crossed the distance between us. "You'll pay for that."

For fuck's sake. Was I the only one fighting the good fight here?

"Eli?" I sat up onto my knees, wiping perspiration off my face. "You forgot to finish one."

"You don't mind taking care of him, do you?" Eli yelled back, with his canines nowhere in sight. He was moving up and down across the floor, his head bowed.

"Why—" I timed my punch against the approaching man's leg for maximum trauma. "—would I?"

The crunch on impact proved a pleasing sound. He stumbled.

I leaped to a standing position and followed up with a kick in his balls, an elbow in his back, and a hard chop against the back of his skull. He, too, slumped down, joining his brother in a deep sleep.

All eight men appeared to have been demons. If Mehmet had sent any vampires of his own to help with the shipment, this confrontation would have had a different outcome.

I cleaned my hands on my sweater. Eli's prey—numbers three and four—were lying in a crumpled stack near a table. Their chests no longer pumped oxygen, it seemed, although I was too far away to be sure. Eli, meanwhile, examined the far end of the barn with his back arched.

The last demon still on his feet took the director down with his body weight alone. Under Lathan's encouragement, he pummeled Vanguard's face without break.

A nasty smile crept onto my lips. So what if the asshole got hurt? His arrogance could do with a reality check.

"Eli?" Mehmet shifted his gaze toward the corner where Eli paced. The kinlord no longer sounded like the strict but kind grandfather. "Stand still for a second and listen."

"Help the director." Eli gestured with both hands at me, then resumed his tour along the wall of the barn. "Go on."

He was looking for something. Unfortunately, that meant that, once again, it was up to me to save the director's hide. I sprinted over and took demon number eight out with a slice to his throat.

Then I turned my back on Vanguard, who was catching his breath in the dirt, where he belonged.

"Eli." The name rattled in Mehmet's throat. "Talk to me."

His hologram, like Lathan's, merged into a thin line of smoke that trailed into separate cubes on the table. The two boxes were made of dark wood, with complicated carvings on their open lids. Guards, possibly. I was familiar only with those made of metal, but my understanding of magical materials was limited.

"I have nothing to say to you." Eli abandoned his hunched posture and glowered at his grand-sire. "But *you* owe me an explanation."

"I owe you nothing. Nothing, boy." Mehmet shut his eyes, his jaw shifting violently. "Fine. Let's start again. Why are you working against me?"

"I'm declaring my independence." Eli leaned his head to the side, as if commiting Mehmet's fragile restraint to memory. "The question is, what are you doing? Working with *that*?"

He shot the nastiest look at Lathan.

"This collaboration couldn't have happened without you." Mehmet raised a heavily ringed finger. "When I confronted Lathan with what I knew of his operation, we came to an understanding."

I moved toward Eli, who stopped me with a shake of his head.

"What kind of understanding?" He inched to his right, into his kinlord's field of view.

"Mehmet, don't you dare." Lathan added a snarl, as if his reputation didn't make him fearsome enough.

"Don't threaten me," Mehmet hurled back. "This is my grandson, and he'll do as I tell him."

Seems their new partnership wasn't built on solid foundations. Centuries of hatred and mistrust were tough to overcome.

"What understanding?" Eli repeated.

"Once we subdue the other five races with Lathan's poison, we will disable the magic between our realms."

"Impossible." Eli's shoulders tensed.

"Not so. I have known how to penetrate the force separating us for months. Your sire proved it can be done. Alone, I lack the power to follow his example, but with Lathan's help, I will succeed." Mehmet smiled proudly.

Eli glared at his grand-sire with incredulous eyes. "And you trust him?"

Hardly the greatest concern at this moment.

"Eli?" I gave a warning growl. "What are you doing?"

Eli bared his canines. "Quiet."

"Lathan and I have entered into a pact that cannot be broken." Mehmet's expression relaxed. "All you need to do is finish what Lathan's people started. Send the boxes across."

"You will poison the children?" Eli retracted his fangs, his tone inquisitive. "Sacrifice them for the greater good?"

The kinlord lifted his chin. "Inferior races. No vampires will die under our rule. Now, my sweet boy. What do you say? Are you ready to rule?"

"You really think you can lure me with power?" Eli gave him the finger. "You crazy old fool."

"Eli!" Mehmet glared, unable to do anything else. "You ungrateful child. I thought Florian was the troublemaker, not you."

"Turns out, my brother and I have more in common than I thought." Eli kicked at the table, which collapsed.

"Control your man!" Lathan shouted.

The cubes tumbled to the ground. Eli stomped on them, and the bright holograms vanished.

"Did you hear? I'm as troublesome as Florian." Eli grinned. "I feel all dirty now."

"I'm sure that feeling will pass." Yet my chuckle died in my throat.

What did Eli's future hold now?

The director moaned. He still lay on the floor in an unnatural position, holding his side. He must have broken something when the other demon toppled him.

Eli turned toward the portal. "How do we close this thing? I've been trying to find a power source but don't even know what I'm looking for."

"No idea." I stepped over my former attacker's unmoving shape to check on the director.

"Crap. This guy's covered in blood." Eli knelt beside one of the portal guards that had been eliminated before we'd arrived, checked for a pulse, and shook his head. "I think it's what's keeping the portal open."

"Come on, Vanguard." I glowered at the demon's pitiful form. "Get up. Fun time's over."

He barely acknowledged me.

"Hey, Eli?" I called. "I think the director's in trouble."

Eli abandoned his search and ran toward me, but stopped in his tracks about fifteen feet away. "I smell blood on his body, too."

I bent over and felt along Vanguard's side until my hand found something warm and wet.

"Shit. He got stabbed." A dark-red stain coated my hand. "Call an ambulance. Quick."

"We can't." Eli slowly reversed back toward the portal. His calm this close to all this blood was only skin-deep. "If we send him to the hospital, he'll be easy prey to Lathan's hit squads."

"What, then?"

Eli had already retrieved his cell phone. "Mina? I need you and Rollo to come out to Lawton's Bridge and— ... I know the site's supposed to be secret. The director's hurt, and you need to patch him up. ... Don't tell me things I already know. Just come."

He ended the conversation, such as it was, and gathered up Lathan's fallen soldiers in one location. He didn't kill them outright. If he kept them alive, we'd be able to squeeze information from them.

"Tell my wife..." Vanguard mumbled. "Tell her I'm sorry."

Oh Christ. I applied pressure to Vanguard's wound to stem the blood flow. My medical knowledge extended to trivia about the plague I remembered from school, which wasn't helpful.

"Tell her yourself." I rolled my eyes. "I don't work for you. Remember?"

He gave a weak, throaty laugh that turned into a cough.

The whooshing background noise ceased, and the glistening portal collapsed unto itself.

"Got it." Eli skipped away from the dead guard's position, keeping his arm tight against his nose.

One less worry for me, because I didn't want him anywhere near blood.

"How did you shut it down?" I squinted at the object in his hand.

"Found a metal disk with lines running across it under the body. Like you did with the picture frame guard earlier, I poked around on it, and the portal closed."

"No-no." I shook my head, even while my hand pressed hard on Vanguard's injury. "I didn't poke at it. *I skillfully and methodically turned off the flux of magic.* Big difference."

"Riiight." He dropped the metal object, which swirled up a thin layer of dust upon impact. "I hear a car. Stay here."

Eli dashed out the door, into the darkness.

As if I'd simply leave the dying director to his fate. He was a conceited bastard without any redeeming features—but he'd stood with us against the kinlords.

Vanguard raised his head by a fraction, then groaned, and let it fall back onto the ground.

"You can't trust the vampire." The director shifted an arm. "Mehmet had plans for Dupree. That tells you everything you need to know."

"I don't think Mehmet's pleased with Eli right now." My hand was drenched in blood, yet I pushed deeper into the wound. "Nor is Lathan with you."

"If I don't die today, I'll die soon enough. Best I can hope for is to reach my family before my kinlord's people do. My only consolation is that your boyfriend's just as dead as I am."

"You're a vile creature." I thrust against his injury until he winced, then eased up.

Hurting Vanguard was satisfactory, but ultimately pointless. Not even killing him would change his personality.

"You might be fucked, but Eli's not alone. Not anymore." I would make sure of that. Whatever Parker's plans for me, Eli would be safe.

"Maybe, but don't underestimate what's coming. I've been planning for this emergency for years." He grimaced and closed his eyes, his voice weakening. "And it's going to get worse. You heard them. I always knew that Lathan would break out of Alethia sooner or later."

Mina charged in with Rollo in tow, and Eli followed behind them with less urgency.

"With luck, you won't be around to witness it." I spitefully squeezed Vanguard's side one last time before turning to Mina. "Any kind of healing or first aid you perform is wasted on him."

Her stern look bounced off the steel door around my heart. No sympathy for assholes—that was my new motto.

"You didn't get yourself into enough trouble tonight?" Rollo asked me as Mina shooed me aside. "Now you're going up against Lathan and Mehmet?"

"We had help." I stood next to Rollo, not far from Vanguard's trembling, wheezing form. "He might not have added muscle, but in spirit, he was encouraging us."

"Shut up, furball," the director murmured.

If he survived this, it would be a miracle. And not one I'd be happy about.

Rollo placed his hand on my shoulder, something he'd never done before.

"I love you, man, but you look like crap." His smile held as much tender worry as honest amusement. "Clean yourself up, or I won't be able to tell which blood on your body is yours once Parker's done with you."

I hadn't forgotten the difficult conversation that lay ahead of me.

"You got this?" Eli pointed behind him at the pile of knocked-out demons. "These guys can't wait to enjoy your alpha's hospitality."

"I got it." Rollo gave him a double thumbs-up. "Once we've made our new guests spill their secrets, they'll get their rest. We're also sending Keely and her wolves to shut down the factory. Your tech guy gave us the address."

Two ruthless guys talking shop. The unconscious demons didn't know the amount of hurt they were in for, but maybe we'd discover more about Lathan's and Mehmet's unholy alliance.

I reeled backward, nearly sagging under my adrenaline crash. The slump came on suddenly. The body could run on its reserves only for so long, and mine had reached its limit.

But my journey wasn't over yet. My reckoning was still to come. I braced my shoulders, inhaled a lungful of oxygen, and slowly regained focus.

Mina worked magic on Vanguard. A white glow cascaded from her flat hands into the demon's body, while her lips moved feverishly. She clearly had a knack for dealing with the not-yet-deceased, too. Her care might just spare me a conversation with the director's wife.

"It's for you." Rollo pressed his cell phone against my ear.

Shit.

"Ali? You okay, man?" Parker's voice snapped my spine straight.

"Hey. Before you say anything, I can explain." Somehow.

"I said, are you okay?"

"Yes. Sorry. Yes, I'm good."

"Rollo and his medical examiner friend have filled me in as much as they could." Even all the way from Custer Fields, Parker's anger carried through the ether and connected to the wolf inside my chest. Such was his power. "Come home."

"I don't know what to say, man." I absorbed Eli's frown, even drew comfort from it, but this was my mess to deal with. "Is Heidi—"

"She's here. We're preparing her." Parker inhaled sharply. "I expect to see you in twenty minutes."

He hung up.

I dropped my head and kicked at the dust under my feet.

"How much trouble are you in?" Eli's breath blew over my neck so close, it brought a pleasant shiver to my spine.

"I don't know yet." I turned toward him, our faces now inches apart. "Guess it's time to face my alpha in person."

A thin line of dried blood ran from the corner of Eli's mouth down to his jaw. "I'll come with you."

"Not a good idea."

"This isn't a debate. We're in this together, remember?"

"I remember." Maybe I'd been hoping he'd say that.

No point denying it. Both his humor and his unfailing loyalty attracted me on a physical level, right down to my wolf. Of course, it helped that he was hot as all hell.

Eli tilted his head to the side. "Another car's coming."

"That would be our people." Rollo snatched back his phone from me. "Now get out of here, you crazy kids."

Eli and I limped toward the exit past four of my men, who met my nods with somber expressions. They'd been told about Heidi, and soon, the rest of the pack would know, too.

We climbed into my car, with Eli at the wheel. He eased my Volvo into a one-hundred-and-eighty-degree maneuver and set off toward Custer Fields.

"About earlier." I massaged my fingers, drinking in the resulting release of tension. "I didn't mean to growl at you."

"Course you did." He smiled softly. "I'd have been disappointed if you hadn't."

"What's going to happen to the IEA now?" I slumped against the door, barely aware of the fields, sidewalks, and buildings we passed.

"That depends on whether Vanguard survives. Mina says it looks worse than it is, but I doubt he'll come back to the office."

"Yeah, probably not." I must have missed that conversation in my haze. "Does that mean you're the director now?"

"I think it's fair to say my time on the IEA's payroll has come to an end as well."

Of course, I'd already guessed as much. "Sorry. That sucks."

"Nah, it wouldn't be the same without Vanguard's constant putdowns anyway."

I rolled my head to my left. Eli's face was no longer as pink as after his feeding, his movements no longer as energetic as when I'd first opened the door to him, but his expression wasn't obscured by a frown anymore either. It might take days for our new reality to become tangible. The last seven hours had passed in a crazy blur. It was a miracle Eli and I had escaped unhurt.

Not everyone had been that lucky.

My car's interior was stained with the director's blood, transferred by my hands, and the seats were dusted with the grime from my fight. No amount of shampoo and detergent would get rid of either. Maybe I shouldn't even try. I'd earned that dirt, every stinking molecule of it.

"Do you think Mehmet's people will come after you?" I stole a glimpse of my equally filthy and scratched-up face in the mirror.

"No."

I lifted my head. "Seriously?"

"I think he'll want to kill me himself. The only question is, will his and Lathan's pact hold long enough for them to make it out of Alethia?"

"You certainly know how to spoil a party." I gave a grim chuckle. "Shouldn't victories feel more triumphant than this?"

"Not if Lathan and Mehmet have anything to say about it."

"Actually, I have a more immediate worry. My alpha's judgement."

The Volvo rounded a corner, with Eli turning the steering

wheel with the same grace that accompanied his usual movements. "Are you scared?" he asked.

"Of Parker? I don't know. He's always been a source of support and guidance for me. Then again, I've never had cause to fear him."

He slowed and rolled up onto the paved drive that led to our house. "We're here."

"Goodie." A sigh punctuated my statement as I tightened my hand around the seat belt buckle.

"Well, we know I'm screwed." Eli parked next to Ivy's Mustang and beamed at me. "Let's find out how much trouble *you're* in."

CHAPTER SEVENTEEN

Passing my friends without talking to them was hard. If I'd been anyone else, more on their level, we would have exchanged hugs and comfort. They knew what Heidi had meant to me, but they would also have heard of my transgressions.

My welcome wasn't helped by Eli's presence. He let the stares bounce off him, but his tense walk belied his apparent confidence. When I'd first entered the IEA's building, I'd headed into enemy territory. Even though he'd mingled with the pack at Florian's bonding ceremony, he would be feeling just as out of place right now.

I led him up the stairs and down the corridor, past the door that carried my name plate, toward Parker's office. I knocked and waited.

In the past, I might have rushed in before my alpha called me, but I would no longer be able to take such liberties.

"Come in," Parker shouted.

I pushed down the handle and eased open the door.

Damn. Ivy wasn't here. Neither was Florian. There was no reason for either to join us for this conversation, of course, but both knew how to diffuse a situation that got too heated. Ivy, in particular, could calm Parker with a touch or even a look.

Parker had a phone pressed to his ear, and he invited us with his eyes to approach. His desk contained stacks of paper that never seemed to go down, no matter how much I pitched in. He'd recently upgraded to two monitors to help him tackle the workload, but until he grew another pair of hands, he was doomed to play catch-up forever.

Eli made a move to sit in one of the two chairs that stood in front of Parker's desk, but a glance from Parker brought him to a hold. Parker wasn't like Vanguard. His threats weren't empty. And unlike lowly me, who brought only the muscles on his body into a fight, my alpha commanded the power of the largest shifter pack in the world and all the magic that accompanied his status. Eli could probably take me out in a few moves, but he'd find his match in Parker—and then some.

"The Mourning takes precedence." Parker ran a hand through his short, dark-blond hair and scribbled a few notes on a piece of paper. "Yes, today. ... Today, I said. ... Only our pack and Keely's."

Would I be invited to the Mourning? I should have been the one organizing the ritual; not Parker. I hid my sweaty palms in my fists, as if my thumping heart didn't already advertise my panic to Eli and Parker. The loss of my job was a foregone conclusion, but the unthinkable scenario was being exiled from the pack. I'd have to give up my room, my friendships, all the ties to my home. Heidi would be interred in my absence, and I'd have to accept my fate because the alternative would mean challenging Parker—and his overwhelming magic power—in a fight to the death.

But if I stayed, what would my life be like then? Would I be demoted to the lowest rank, punished to perform the most menial of duties? Would I still be allowed to see Eli? How could I protect him against Mehmet's hit squad if I no longer had any clout in my pack?

Parker's conversation had turned one-sided, with him being the one who listened. An occasional nod or hum revealed his waning interest in what the other person had to say.

"That sounds good." Parker drummed his fingers on his desk. "Do that. If you have questions, talk to Jim."

I winced but immediately regained control over my muscles. Standing in for Parker—that used to be my job. Jim had often claimed he'd make a better second, although he'd never challenged me directly. Now, I'd served him his promotion on a platter.

And yet, I couldn't have acted in any other way. If I hadn't teamed up with Eli, Heidi's death would most likely remain unavenged, and thousands of kin children in Alethia would be marked for death.

Parker tapped the display and placed his cell on his desk. He lifted his head and let his gaze slide past Eli to settle on my dirty, bloody face.

I swallowed. Hard. A painful, wretched thing to do when your mouth was dry and your throat had narrowed to the size of a needle.

He didn't smile. Didn't ask us to sit.

"Tell me." Two words, spoken without audible anticipation.

I took a deep breath. Parker preferred clear and to-the-point reports, and I wasn't one to embellish.

"I opened the door late last night to find Heidi's body on our doorstep." My legs, tired after the fights and from a lack of rest, were cramping, but I would not sit without permission. "Eli discovered her first. He claimed she was one of many victims of an unknown serial killer. He gave me a choice: inform my alpha, or join his investigation and utilize the IEA's resources to bring the killer to justice."

"You picked the IEA." The irritation was there, in Parker's tone, but he didn't let it erupt. Not yet.

My grief had coiled tight around my heart, whereas he'd be feeling Heidi's absence in his bones. Neither of us would give into our emotions until no secrets remained.

"I picked the option that had the better prospects of succeeding." I jerked my chin toward Eli's still unmoving figure. "Our pack knew nothing of these other events. It would have taken us weeks to catch up."

"Go on." Parker grabbed his pen and held it tight.

"A sandman called Max Hoffmann had carried Heidi's body to our doorstep, but it was a demon called Jack Gdansk who ultimately killed her."

"He's the mess that Rollo dragged in?"

"Yes." I gave a terse smile. "Rollo has been excellent from the moment I first called him."

"Noted." He barely moved.

Maybe I'd hoped for his eyes to twitch or for a subtle nod of encouragement, yet neither materialized.

"Heidi was a victim of Jack's experiments. Even as his research was ongoing, his company produced large batches of poisoned candy bars to ship to Alethia. He..." For the first time, my account faltered.

Whatever I'd done, Parker was my best friend. And Ivy was his happiness. The mere mention of Lathan's name would shatter what remaining calm my alpha possessed because it would drive the fear back into her heart.

"To absolutely no one's surprise, Lathan was behind everything." Eli's voice was as matter-of-fact as mine had been up to this point.

"Ivy's gonna love that." The pain that underlay Parker's words spoke of the depth of his feelings for her.

"Oh, she's strong." Eli raised his eyebrows. "Besides, she won't dwell on those news for long once she finds out that this isn't the end of the clusterfuck of betrayals and conspiracies we've uncovered."

"Sometimes I think you shouldn't be allowed to speak," I murmured. "What Eli means is that Mehmet, the vampire kinlord, is working with Lathan now."

"You serious?" Parker's pen missiled across the desk, clanged off his water glass, and fell to the floor. "Fucking hell."

"My sentiments exactly." Eli tucked one hand into his pocket. "We've foiled their initial plan. As far as we know, not one poisoned candy bar crossed into Alethia, but if their cooperation survives this setback, they might succeed in breaking free of Alethia soon. Apparently, Mehmet knows how."

"Let's not go there." Parker waved off. "Not today. How about you two? Are you injured?"

"No," Eli and I replied in unison.

"Okay, good. Then I suggest you get some sleep." Parker's pitch normalized. "You'll want to be alert for the Mourning. We start at nine sharp."

"With all respect, I'd rather get my punishment over with now." I lowered my head. "Don't make me wait another day."

Eli moved toward me, his body lacking the comforting heat I needed, but he made up for it by ensuring his arm touched mine.

"Punishment? You're not in trouble, Ali." Parker's words made little sense. "You did well. I'm proud of the way you handled yourself. Get that?"

I raised my gaze. "But I worked with the IEA."

"You worked with Florian's brother." He let out a long stream of air. "Let's not fool ourselves. I'm not thrilled about this, but I trust you acted with caution. End of story. Now, go get some sleep. That's an order. We'll talk more once we've all had time to absorb what happened."

My heart stilled. My muscles slackened. How was I not on my way into exile?

"May I come?" Eli asked. "To the Mourning?"

I opened my mouth, but even if I'd suddenly rediscovered my voice, I wouldn't have objected. Parker could speak for himself.

"We'd be glad to have you." Parker got up and walked around the table, arm held aloft. "Thank you for everything."

He and Eli shook hands.

"My pleasure." Eli beamed.

Parker moved over to me, gave me a playful slap on my cheek, before wrapping his arms around me. "Punishment," he whispered before giving a short chuckle. "Seriously."

The touch of my alpha came with an indefinable source of tranquility, as if my body was renewing itself, cell by cell, and my blood was flowing cleaner and faster than ever.

Too soon, he let go.

"Get some rest, my friend." He patted my shoulder.

I slowly nodded and made my way out of his office, weighed down by fatigue and grief, yet Parker's "my friend" had buoyed my soul.

"That went better than expected." Eli's voice yanked me back to reality. "If you're up for it, I know a fly place with beer, a warm fire, clean clothes, and a shower."

I hurried after him down the stairs. "You do know some pretty cool places."

"You have no idea."

We left the house by the door that had started the worst and best day of my life, passed my Volvo, and headed down the drive and across the road to Eli's home.

The sky shone a very light blue onto us, with only a few dark clouds in the distance. The ground would soon be dry; dry enough for Heidi's interment.

He led me upstairs to his rooms, where everything was as we'd left it. Only the fire had burned down to a mellow glow, but another log took care of that.

I brushed ash off my clothes as if that made any difference.

"Go take a shower." Eli opened the bathroom door for me. "I'll use the one down the hall."

I was lucky that my bedroom at home came with an adjoining bathroom, yet it was nothing as luxurious as Eli's. The IEA didn't pay him enough to afford oversized showers and expensive cars, but it was no secret that his sister was a bestselling author and a shrewd investor. Yet despite the family's wealth, I suspected Eli would also feel at home in a cheap house share.

As soon as the warming jet of water massaged my aching body, my spirit regenerated. For the first time, I'd gone against my instincts and not played it safe, and I'd actually achieved something. Thousands of kids would be alive next week because we'd stopped the candy bars from getting into Alethia. Not to overlook, we'd caught Heidi's killer—and it was barely eight o'clock.

I came out of the shower just as a hand reached into the bathroom, holding a new set of clothes.

"Thanks." I placed them on the toilet seat.

"No problem." Eli's arm lingered.

I stood rigid in place. Waiting.

"Hurry up. The beer's getting warm." The hand disappeared and the door closed.

I exhaled sharply. What had I thought was going to happen? That Eli would swoop in and kiss me like no man had kissed me before? When had I turned into a teenage girl?

Dressed in Eli's clothes and feeling clean for the first time in hours, I joined him in his room. My jeans were of a wider fit than before. This time it was the T-shirt that had to stretch to accommodate my chest.

His blond hair was combed straight, framing his blood-free face, and his eyes were clear and bright. Our dirty clothes from earlier still lay scattered across the room, as did the documents from our investigation. They'd be evidence now. Once the kin of all races discovered Lathan's and Mehmet's attempted crime, the lines would be drawn. They'd have to pick sides.

At any other time, the urge to tidy up would overcome me, but Eli's scent of ocean and spice took my mind off the mess.

I patted my head, then my neck.

"What's wrong?" Eli passed me a can then sat on the hardwood floor with his back against the sofa.

"Nothing. Just not used to the short hair yet." Once again, I ran my fingers through what remained once the barber had been done with it. "Florian's idea, of course, although my fault for following his advice."

I'd lost inches that day, yet the 'new me' I'd been hoping for hadn't materialized. Just the same me with a cold neck.

"Ah, Florian again. Of course." Eli's tone was hard to place.

"We're still friends." I took a seat next to him and opened my can. "That won't change."

"No, maybe not. But isn't it weird seeing him and his girl all the time?"

"Not really. They truly are happy together. It's nice."

Eli shoved aside a stack of documents that separated us. "You are totally over him then?"

"I told you, yes. I have been for a while."

"But?"

How well he'd gotten to know me in just a few hours.

"I miss the closeness." I held the cool can against my forehead. "Sharing an emotional connection with another person, that's not something I thought I'd ever do. Look at me. Indonesian parents. Gay. Werewolf."

"Cute smile, though." He bumped my shoulder with his.

"There's that, yes." I flashed one, just for him.

"So it's the connection you miss. I can get behind that."

"What if it's never going to happen again?"

"Oh man, that's how you wanna play this?" Eli stretched his legs flat on the floor and groaned. "I wasn't my sire's favorite son, and I wasn't his little girl. Mehmet was the first to show an interest, and look how that turned out. As for the rest of my family? Florian's hooked up with Keely. My sister's doing her thing and hardly comes home now. Maybe that's for the better because who needs ties when you have to go on the lam because there's a bounty on your head?"

"You win." I elbowed him gently. "The Most Pathetic Award goes to you."

"I'll drink to that." He raised his can.

I didn't lift mine. "Parker isn't going to kick me out, and as long as I have a place in my pack, you will have one, too."

"Don't make promises you can't keep." Eli lowered his hand. "Parker—"

"Parker has this rule: Those who fight with us are pack. You fought by my side."

"You think you have room for one more vampire?"

"We'll *make* room." I finally waved my can in the air. "Do you want to drink to that maybe?"

"Sure."

We clinked our cans together.

The room was warming up, but whether through the fire, the beer, or the company, I couldn't tell.

"I like BBQ-flavored hot sauce." Eli chuckled. "I'm crazy about it."

"What?" I shot him a sideways glance.

"For you, it's sweet soy sauce. I can't get enough of BBQ hot sauce."

"Duly noted." I brushed my thumb over my jeans. Over *Eli's* jeans on *my* legs. "You know, you don't need the IEA. We made a good team. Maybe there's more crime for us to bust in Silverton."

"You wanna play Murtaugh to my Riggs?"

I held my hand up to my face. "I'm not as dark as Murtaugh."

"I'm not as dark as Riggs either." Eli laughed. "I have a vampire's complexion."

The large TV on the wall was the only indulgence in this room. The bookshelf lay empty except for a vase with artificial flowers. The little décor that there was had probably been his sister's doing. Even though the space gave hardly anything away about the man by my side, I felt like I'd known him for years.

"And you're definitely over Florian?" he asked. "No lingering doubts?"

Something in his tone made my heart lurch. "I told you, no doubts."

"That means you're on the market."

"If you mean I can be bought, then hell yeah. A meal and a beer, and I'm yours."

Eli shifted his body to face me. "You have a beer and potato chips. What do you say?"

Was he serious?

Through the large window, the sun continued its journey against the horizon, promising to hide the ugliness of the last few hours inside its glorious light. Still, a hint of nostalgia for the darkness crept into my chest. The night had not brought Heidi back to life, but in a way, it had restored mine. For the first time, I'd earned my position inside my pack. None of that would have been possible without the encouragement of my new favorite vampire.

"I'll throw in a pizza if it helps." The blue in Eli's eyes gave way to the black of his pupils.

I pushed a streak of hair from his face. "Sounds like an offer I can't refuse."

Eli leaned forward, and his mouth found mine with lethal precision. I put my can down and then slid my hand around his neck, gathering him closer.

We were partners. I'd put my life on the line on his promise, and he'd come through, every fucking minute of the night. This man who'd kept propping me up when I was ready to fall—this man was now kissing the blazing hell out of me.

Shit. Could I be this lucky?

The up-and-down sensation in my stomach was new. The sudden need for his lips struck me with a visceral force.

He moaned softly, emboldening me. I dragged him closer to feel his chest against mine, to drink in his oddly cool breath, to brush my nose across his rugged cheek. His fresh scent unleashed a torrent of need inside me. When our tongues met, sparks short-circuited my brain.

How had we got here? This thing between us, this amazing, stomach-tickling connection we shared, had come out of nowhere. I hadn't planned for it, yet it felt earned. Deserved.

Eli searched my T-shirt for an entry point and reached underneath. Not to grab me—just to touch me. This I knew, because I understood.

The loneliness. The need to connect. The being different.

I understood it all.

He retreated and brushed his finger over my lips. "I'm not Florian. And I'm not my sister. I don't play around with people, and I don't date casually."

Every one of his words stoked a fire in my guts. I kept my hand on his neck, kissed the corner of his mouth.

"Stop comparing yourself to others. Trust me when I say I'm glad you're not your brother, and I'm ecstatic you're not your sister." My smile grew with each heartbeat. "And I don't do casual either."

"As long as we're clear on that." He took my head between both his hands and dragged me back into his kiss.

A kiss so demanding, it shook me to my core, because it announced a new chapter in my life, a new adventure greater even than the one I'd just had. What I knew for certain was that with Eli by my side, change might be easier than I thought.

This was book 3 of The Silverton Chronicles. I hope you enjoyed it. Have you tried any of my other books yet? Read on for the blurbs.

MOON PROMISE

The Wild Pack

All her life, Kensi has dreamed of being an alpha werewolf. The trouble is, she can't shift—and no one must know. Her plan B? Offering her talents as a private eye to the Wild Pack. If she can locate their missing werewolf, they're bound to support her claim to lead.

Stubborn and searing-hot Drake is assigned to be her guide. His constant push for dominance threatens the investigation from the start, yet far more dangerous are his mercury eyes. They watch her all the time, breaking down her defenses bit by bit. Unless she finds a way to control her growing feelings, he could uncover her secret before she even gets close to solving her case.

But when the missing girl turns up dead, Drake's story unravels...

DIVIDE AND CONQUER

Champions of Elonia

How the hell does a physicist like Lea Daniels get dragged into a fight to defend a magical kingdom? A lousy prophecy, that's how. Grappling with her new reality, Lea must entrust her safety to Elonian warrior Nieve, whose kick-ass powers blatantly defy the laws of nature.

Nieve, for her part, isn't exactly thrilled either about her role as a mentor to a "chosen one" who can't tell a sword from a hairbrush. They've barely had time to cover the rules of Elonian light magic when they're attacked from the shadows—where only the enemy dares walk.

Somehow, the mismatched duo must protect Seattle, the world, and the realm beyond against the Shade king and his cut-throat army. The good news is, they're not alone. The bad news is that, as new allies assemble to join their cause, it quickly becomes clear everyone has an agenda.

BOOKS BY CARMEN FOX

The Silverton Chronicles

Guarded

Bound

Hidden

Trapped – Free download for newsletter subscribers:

https://dl.bookfunnel.com/pyzqppmb32

The Wild Pack

Moon Promise

Champions of Elonia

Divide and Conquer

Hide and Seek

Bait and Switch

Also available

Conversations with the Dead

A Knight's Quest

ABOUT THE AUTHOR

USA Today Bestselling Author Carmen Fox lives in the south of England with her beloved tea maker and a stuffed sheep called Fergus. She writes about smart women with sassitude and guys with an edge, and will chase that plot twist, no matter how elusive.

Website: www.carmen-fox.com

ACKNOWLEDGEMENTS

There are many people to thank, as always. My wonderful editors and proofreaders, especially Sharon G. for reading the book *twice* (and she isn't even a fan of the genre!). My newsletter readers for advising me on what works and what doesn't. Among them, Mary B., who went above and beyond to help me improve my plot's flow. Ana for her stunning cover. And as always, my mother.

If you're a fan of The Silverton Chronicles, I want to thank you for sticking with me. You may have noticed a change in the 'feel' of my books. That's because writers evolve. Readers do, too. Since Guarded, you may have accepted a new job or new responsibilities, paid off a chunk of your mortgage, or have welcomed new family members.

As for me, I use fewer metaphors and 'big words,' my plots have simplified, and my style is smoother than it was in the beginning. What hasn't changed is my voice. I'm not a funny person, but luckily, my characters often are.

Hopefully you will forgive my early mistakes—and the ones I'm still making. Let's keep growing together.